LIAHONA

The Compass's Story

Book 5 of

The TRACKERS SERIES

MICKEY MORNINGGLORY

Patent Print Books

Panama City Beach, Florida

This is a work of fiction, and the views expressed herein are the sole responsibility of the author. The characters, places, and incidents portrayed in this book are products of the author's imagination, and any resemblance to actual persons, living or dead, or actual events or locales, is entirely coincidental.

LIAHONA: The Compass's Story
The Trackers Series, Book 5

Published by PATENT PRINT BOOKS
www.patentprintbooks.com
PATENT PRINT BOOKS and the fingerprint colophon
are registered trademarks of PATENT PRINT BOOKS

Copyright ©2019 by Mickey MorningGlory
Cover design ©2019 by M. Middleton
Edited by Ann W. Carns

First Edition: October 2019

Printed in the United States of America

ISBN 978-0-9850731-4-5
Library of Congress Control Number: 2019911259

10   9   8   7   6   5   4   3   2   1

In memory of
Dr. Wilbur A. Middleton ~
My inspiration, my hero, my father.

FOREWORD

The number seven has always been special in literature and history. What if you discover you are the seventh son of a seventh son? What potential wisdom, force, or power have you inherited from your ancestors? How can you learn to express yourself as a tracker? And will you serve as a force for good or succumb to the selfish lure of evil?

A growing, crowded, exciting society can be found almost anywhere in present-day America. This author produces human characters who live, love, and compete for power and success in the pluralistic State of Florida. Power politics, big-time sports, and mystical dimensions of extra-sensory time travel capture the reader's interest. Unexpected themes drawn from ancient value systems, from Hispanic culture, and from Native American intrigue permeate the more normal local, secular culture in Florida's capital city and its environs. Every reader will identify with the pathos of vicious kidnapping, of fortunes made and lost, and of intimate love so close and yet so far away.

Mickey MorningGlory writes in a crisp, sharp, and brisk tempo. Her compelling characters capture your attention and the suspense of their intricate involvements, both virtuous and vicious, will keep you glued to the page until you arrive at the surprising conclusion. And then you will quickly ask for the next installment in this well-planned series which promises to continue to draw us into the amazing adventures of these exciting trackers.

~ Robert G. Newman, Ph.D.
A.J. Humphreys Professor of Religion
The University of Charleston

CONTENTS

PREFACE

LIAHONA, the fifth book in *The Trackers Series,* is Lee Thistleseed's story. Very little time elapsed after Graham and Shine left the Navajo Reservation before every round object I saw became the ancient *Liahona* compass in my eyes. I suppose it was calling out to alert me to Lee's imminent quest.

~ Mickey

ACKNOWLEDGMENTS

I want to thank those who had a part in the inspiration and completion of this book (in alphabetical order):

Angela J., Ann C., Felicia B., Guy P., Jacki T., Jan V., Katie M., Margaret K., Matt K., Mike C., Robert N., Stephen N., Steve N., Wayne B., my editor, my publisher, and especially my family.

INTRODUCTION

"And it came to pass that as my father arose in the morning, and went forth to the tent door, to his great astonishment he beheld upon the ground a round ball of curious workmanship; and it was of fine brass. And within the ball were two spindles; and the one pointed the way whither we should go into the wilderness."

~ 1 Nephi 16:10,
The Book of Mormon

NEW ORLEANS, LA~JUNE~1993

ON A BACKSTREET IN NEW ORLEANS, three men gathered in the dark of the night.

"The hour is nigh," the youngest said.

"He is ready for the quest," the oldest said.

"The Compass is revealed," the middle one said.

*   *   *

In his Tallahassee, Florida, home, Liahona Thistleseed stands before his front door. The bell announces the arrival of expected and unexpected guests. Lee finds that his hand is sweaty, and his fingers slip off the door handle. He wipes his palm on his pants and reaches forward again, this time grasping the knob more firmly. Behind Lee stands Wren, his Cherokee wife, silently wringing a damp handkerchief.

Opening the door, Lee is face to face with a man in his

1

late thirties or perhaps early forties—John Revell, Mission President for the Tallahassee Stake of the Church of Jesus Christ of Latter-day Saints—the Mormons. John gives the tall Mohawk Indian a hesitant smile, and then he steps forward to shake hands.

"Brother Thistleseed, it's good to see you," John says.

"Thank you for coming, President Revell. This is my wife, Wren," Lee says.

"Sister Thistleseed. Very nice to meet you," John says.

Wren nods miserably. This is not a good day for her. She looks past the man toward the burgundy van sitting in the circular front driveway.

"He's fine, folks. Please don't worry. I'll explain everything momentarily, but I want you to know that it's OK. These things happen sometimes," John says.

"I don't know what to say," Lee says.

"Some missionaries come home because they're homesick or just can't handle the mission field. Your son Jubal had honorable reasons for leaving early," John says. "Let me get him, and he can tell you." He descends the steps and opens the front passenger door of the van.

The young man steps out of the vehicle and stands blinking in the summer sunlight. He still wears his dark suit, white shirt, black tie, and his plastic name tag which reads "Elder Thistleseed." He glances up at his concerned parents, fearing the worst. But their faces soften, and he knows there

2

are no judgments; his parents love him and trust him.

Jubal steps to the passenger door and pulls it open. Reaching inside, he withdraws a young woman of eighteen. She is slender as a reed and nearly as tall as Jubal. She wears a wrap-around skirt of light blue cotton muslin embroidered with lime-green yarn flowers. It falls just above her feet, which are thrust into bright chartreuse flip flops. Her loose-fitting sleeveless gauzy top matches the skirt, and her head is wrapped with matching fabric in a turban-like arrangement.

Clutching the young man's hand, she shyly regards the two strangers on the porch. Jubal pulls her closer. Her skin is smooth, polished mahogany, and her eyes mimic the black star sapphire gemstones which hang from her tiny earlobes.

"Mom, Dad, this is Sali Mata Jacomba. I mean, Sali Mata Thistleseed. She is my wife," Jubal says.

Wren steps forward with wide eyes. The girl looks at her with a tentative, but proud expression, waiting for a reaction from her new in-laws.

"Oh, Jubal," Wren whispers, "what have you done? She is barely more than a child." Then, she smiles warmly, descends the steps, and embraces the girl.

The change in Sali Mata is spectacular. A radiant smile lights up her face, and she returns the embrace with a laugh. The ice is broken, and Lee also comes down to the driveway to shake his son's hand, pulling him in for a strong hug.

When Lee backs up, he notices another set of dark eyes

3

in the backseat. Reaching in, his hand is clasped by a smaller hand. A young boy of ten hops out and gives the adults the full view of his brilliant white teeth.

"Bonjour! Bonjour!" the child shouts, grinning.

"French?" Lee asks.

"It's their second language," John explains.

Sali Mata points at the boy. "Arfang," she says.

"His name is Arfang. He's her little brother. All the rest of her family—parents and siblings—are dead. Murdered because they converted," Jubal says, his voice breaking.

"And now you know the rest of the story," John says. "He baptized them, and he rescued them. Why don't we go in and talk?"

The family begins moving up the steps, but they are ambushed by the two youngest Thistleseeds, twelve-year-old Chenaniah and nine-year-old Shelly. The children grab the newcomers' hands and pull them out to the back yard to jump on the trampoline. Jubal continues into the house.

Inside, John explains the dangers of the villagers converting to Christianity. "Often, a raiding party is organized to exterminate the new converts. Such was the case with Sali Mata and Arfang. They climbed a mango tree and hid out in the leafy branches for two days. Jubal found them in the tree and took them to Senegal. He married Sali Mata and was intent on bringing her and Arfang to America. We arranged for special circumstances passports and visas. It was all done very

4

quickly because the three of them were in danger," John says.

Lee is silent for once, mulling over this information. His concentration is broken by a breathless Shelly running in through the back door.

"Hey Bill. You better come out. Your new wife had a stick in her dress, and she jumped off the trampoline with it and was walking around the yard holding it between her hands. And now, her little brother is on his knees digging a hole in the grass where she pointed the stick," she says.

The four adults are met outside by Kenny, who is holding a shovel. "Here, Dad. You're gonna need this. Dig where he's already started the hole," he says.

Lee takes the shovel and jabs it into the ground. After a few shovels full of earth, he sees an object buried in the dirt. Arfang claps his hands excitedly and points at it. Lee bends down and unearths the thing, holding it in his hands. Taking Wren's damp handkerchief, he wipes off the dirt. They all stand in a circle looking at the strange item.

It is an object of curious workmanship, circular in shape, about five inches in diameter, and rather like a ball or a bowl with an open cover. The rounded central top of the cover is held in place by 12 tiny rods in a zig-zag pattern—six points attached to the top, and six points attached to the middle of the bowl-shaped area. Within the bowl are more zig-zag rods.

Suspended in the center of the ball are two horizontal rods, each about the size and shape of a man's finger. They sit one atop the other and can be viewed through the open sides of the upper hemisphere. As Lee holds the object, the rods move freely in a clockwise/counterclockwise motion.

The color inside and out is a bright golden yellow, and it brilliantly reflects the sun. Upon closer inspection, Lee can see it is made of brass.

"*Liahona*," John says quietly.

"It *is* a *Liahona*," Kenny says excitedly. "It might be THE *Liahona*."

"I don't think..." Lee says warily.

"Yes, I believe the boy is right. Buried for centuries, I'm almost sure you have found the ancient *Liahona*, the compass of Lehi," John says.

"I *am* right. I hope you're rested up, Dad. It looks like you have another trip to make," Kenny says.

Lee sighs. Kenny must be in contact with Luna, his telepathic friend from Central America. "What does Luna say now, son?" he asks his gifted son.

"She says you have to leave in three days. You've got to take Graham and Dane with you. I can't go because I'm not old enough, and neither can Noah. It must be four grown men. Oh, yeah. The fourth man is you, Mr. Revell," Kenny says.

*   *   *

Hundreds of miles away, my eyes fly open, and I stare at nothing. I do not know the young girl or her brother, but I know her husband. He is the brother of my friend, Chenaniah.

I am Luna—short for *Ojos del Luna* (as my village family calls me); *Hvresse Torwv* (as my Creek Indian mother calls me). Both names mean the same—Moon Eyes. My blue eyes are almost white, and Mother says that is why I am blind. But when I play my flute, I can see in my dream travels. I often travel great distances, and the world is vivid and colorful, with keen sensory perceptions of sound and smell.

I am a "Story Keeper." I remember in great detail what I see on my journeys. The stories I tell are not mine, but I keep them in my memory always, as do I keep all the other stories related to this group of people whose lives intersect mine in a strange and unexplainable way.

This one is his—the Compass's story. It begins the day my friend's brother brings home a wife from Africa.

CHAPTER ONE
<u>WEDNESDAY, 1993</u>

LIAHONA "LEE" THISTLESEED GINGERLY HOLDS THE BALL in his hands and studies it. He trembles slightly. As the Mohawk leader of the elite clairvoyant Trackers Team—a group of Native American Indians from different tribes who track missing persons and criminals with their minds—it is not a sensation he has often felt. Normally, he is stalwart and steady, brave in the face of danger, and level-headed in conflicts. Lee is the peacekeeper of his family, his colleagues, his team. Tonight, however, he is simply not himself.

The day began with the surprising arrival of his middle son Jubal and a newly acquired family. That is something Lee will have to reflect on later. At this very moment, his attention is commanded by the foreign object in his hands.

Lee is an elder in The Church of Jesus Christ of Latter-day Saints—commonly known as Mormons. The object he holds—albeit impossible for him to conceive—is the *Liahona*, from which, coincidently, his name comes. It is an ancient compass described in the Book of Mormon, a book of scripture important to his faith that is used in conjunction with the Bible.

Although Lee is a lifelong member who treasures his church's teachings and follows the tenets of his religion obediently, he is having trouble wrapping his logical mind around the possibility that this…thing…in his hands is the actual artifact of which he has read and studied for as long as he has been in the Church. Furthermore, the very idea that it has been buried in his own backyard seems too much to bear.

Lee sets the object on the desk and leans back in his chair. Consulting his well-worn scriptures, he once more reads the description in the chapter he has highlighted.

"*And it came to pass that as my father arose in the morning, and went forth to the tent door, to his great astonishment he beheld upon the ground a round ball of curious workmanship; and it was of fine brass. And within the ball were two spindles; and the one pointed the way whither we should go into the wilderness,*" he reads aloud.

A round ball of fine brass with two inner spindles. That fits the description, but I can't be sure this is not someone's homemade interpretation, he thinks.

He thumbs to another chapter in the Book and finds a passage as if in answer to his unspoken question.

9

"*And behold, there cannot any man work after the manner of so curious a workmanship. And behold, it was prepared to show unto our fathers the course which they should travel in the wilderness. And it did work for them according to their faith in God; therefore, if they had faith to believe that God could cause that those spindles should point the way they should go, behold, it was done,*" he reads.

"And if they didn't have faith, the *Liahona* didn't work," Kenny says from the doorway.

Lee lifts his head up to see his youngest son standing against the door watching him intently.

"That's what it says in the chapter written by the prophet Alma, Dad. I looked it up. It says the people didn't exercise their faith and diligence, and they tarried in in the wilderness because of their transgressions," Kenny says. "Aren't transgressions like sins?"

"Yes, Chenaniah. When one transgresses, he is doing something wrong," Lee confirms.

"Yeah, that's what I thought. So, if I get this right, you gotta have faith and diligence and don't sin or it won't work," Kenny says.

Lee nods and pulls one side of his mouth up in a half-smile. "You are right, as usual, son," he concedes.

"So, Luna tells me that it *will* work for you, and it's a really important journey you're taking. She says it's kinda like a life and death thing, only not *your* life or death, which is good

10

because I don't want you to be in danger, you know, like we were in New Mexico when the, um, when the monsters came," he says, shifting from foot to foot.

Lee nods soberly, remembering the recent disturbing events quite clearly.

In May, just after his oldest daughter Shinehah married Graham Skysong—the clairaudient member of the Trackers Team—the newlyweds found themselves engaged in a battle against a serial killer who started his spree by murdering Graham's father. The man used an aberration of the old medicine man's own Blessing Way song to bring a sand painting of the ouroboros—the snake eating its tail—to life. The painting, which featured five snakes in total, killed ten people in Graham's hometown on the Navajo Reservation in Little Water, New Mexico before they located him.

Lee and his young son Kenny traveled to New Mexico to help Graham solve the murders. Little did they know they would become a major part of an epic battle in which their own lives were put in grave danger.

The killer attacked Lee's and Graham's families with sand paintings of six ancient mythological monsters straight from age-old Navajo legends. To fight the monsters, Kenny and his sister Shine, along with Graham's sister Dee and her young son Gilly, had to take part in spiritual and physical combat against horrifying deadly creatures of sand which were brought to life by the corrupted song. Portraying the four warriors of the legends, Shine, Dee, Kenny, and Gilly emerged victorious in destroying the monsters, but not without exposing themselves to great bodily harm.

Lee scans his young son's face and sees some signs of residual trauma. It is not something the boy will ever forget.

"Your Luna is quite something, son. Please give her my thanks for setting your mind at ease," Lee says.

"Oh, yeah, well, she knows, Dad," Kenny replies, "but, tell me something. It says that those people tarried in the wilderness. Doesn't *tarried* mean *wandered*, like Moses and the people of Egypt? Why would you be wandering? I mean, you have your clairvoyant gift of direction, Graham has his clairaudient gift of super good hearing, and Dane has his clairscent gift of smell. And I know you have faith and diligence. So why would you guys wander? I just don't get that."

"*Tarried* means *waited*. *To tarry* means *to wait*. That is not quite the same as wandering," Lee says.

"Luna says she hears people say, '*I would tarry*.' So that's like '*I would wait*,' huh? Still don't get it," Kenny says.

"She says, '*I would tarry*?' Is that exactly what she says? Not '*I am waiting*,' but '*I would tarry*.' Is that what she says?" Lee asks frowning.

"Yep. '*I would tarry*.' She says it over and over," he says, shrugging his shoulders, "like how they talk in the Bible, you know?"

12

"I have no idea why, but, if Luna says it, it must be so. She has been right thus far. Someone is evidently waiting. Maybe that is what this journey with the *Liahona* is all about," Lee ponders.

"Maybe so. And, Dad, she also says for you to '*be mindful of the unseen*,' whatever that means," Kenny says yawning. "Man, I'm tired! I'm going to bed. Crazy day today. Bill comes home from Africa with a wife. I've got a new sister-in-law, and I don't know what you'd call Arfang. I'm just going to call him my new brother. You find the *Liahona* in the back yard. Crazy day."

Kenny suddenly propels himself forward and envelopes Lee with his arms. "I love you, Dad. I really, really do love you a lot. Good night." Turning, he races up the stairs, leaving Lee Thistleseed with his mouth agape and a tear escaping his eye.

*   *   *

Just after midnight—while the Thistleseeds slept in Tallahassee—the tide of people on the beer-scented streets of New Orleans continued to ebb and flow. Music poured into the night from every direction in an ongoing juxtaposition of bouncy jazz, bawdy piano bar, and hard rock. Voices punctuated the music, some singing drunkenly, others arguing in heavily accented patois, many laughing riotously.

Near the harbor, a dark, muscular man of Middle Eastern or perhaps Native American descent lingered in the darkness, hidden within the shadows of the night, alongside the doorway to a floating casino.

"I would tarry," he whispered. He was the oldest of his companions, and his given name was Shemnon, a Hebrew word which meant oil or fatness, neither of which accurately described him. But the man had not used that name in many years. In France he had been known as Jean Non; in Ireland he had been Shaun Noone; in the bayou, he had answered to Sammy John.

He called himself Jim now. It was easier for people to say and much safer, with times being what they were and the panic over foreign terrorists. Jim was safe; Jim was American. Jim could blend in; Shemnon could not.

Jim kept his eyes on the target as he surveilled him from the open doorway. The man strolled through the *Casino Rock Island*, which was tied up at the dock after the latest gaming cruise. It was quaintly styled like a riverboat, with curved decks, decorative *fleur de lis* ornaments, an abundance of windows, and a huge paddlewheel that continued to churn the murky waters. Jim had been trailing the man in New Orleans since yesterday when they were aboard the *Star Casino* on the south shore of Lake Ponchartrain. The target was immensely fond of the offshore floating gambling casinos.

Jim's assigned target was a distinguished man about 60 years old, with a full head of striking white hair brushed back from his forehead. His angular face was tan and lined with barely noticeable creases at his dark brown eyes, full mouth, and reconstructed nose. He allowed himself one blemish in an otherwise flawless face, and that was a tiny gap between his top front teeth, but he felt the slight imperfection put people more at ease.

At well over six feet tall, he was easily spotted in a crowd, as much for his height as for his bearing: he was physically fit, with erect posture and a head held high with self-assurance. He walked jauntily with a rolling lope, long legs striding out confidently. His hands were smooth, the fingers long and tapering. They were gambler's hands, but they were also strong hands, skilled hands...doctor's hands.

The ringing sounds of the one-armed bandits inside the riverboat casino and the raucous shouts of the clientele were loud in Jim's ears. *What a noisy world it has become,* he thought. He watched as Doctor—for the target was, indeed, a gifted and successful plastic surgeon—stood amidst the cacophony and leveled his perfect head left and right. Then, he snapped his attention back to the left and strode purposefully to a vacant slot machine. Jim entered the boat unseen and moved closer. He knew what came next.

Doctor put a silver dollar into his chosen slot machine and pulled the handle. He repeated this action five more times in rapid succession, barely looking at the spinning dials of lemons, cherries, and plums. Then, he changed it up and pumped four silver dollars in, thrusting a plastic bucket

15

beneath the coin return opening before yanking the lever.

The one-armed bandit gave up its plunder. Bells clanged rapidly in a high-pitched staccato, and a red light above the machine revolved brightly, signaling a significant win. Jim could see from his vantage point that Doctor had hit the jackpot. Flashing golden dollar signs were aligned in all four directions—vertical, horizontal, and both diagonals.

Inside the gambling riverboat, other money-seeking patrons materialized amid cheers and applause to see the big winner. The machine spit out silver dollars like projectile vomit, and Doctor filled two buckets before it stopped. An attendant in full riverboat regalia of crimson brocade vest, black satin cravat, white shirt, gold cufflinks, black trousers, and spats, no less, appeared at Doctor's side. He touched his arm and escorted him to the cashier's cage where the big winner could collect the rest of his jackpot in cash, check, or voucher. Doctor chose cash. He always did.

Jim took a quick look at the now vacant machine and read the payout: $11,000. Then, he closely followed Doctor as he strode out of the riverboat and down to the French Quarter.

Doctor avoided the bars where customers in various states of inebriation flocked. Instead, he stuck to the middle of the street, which was cordoned off and rendered impassible by automobiles due to the nightly throng of foot traffic. From his position, he had a good view of the balconies that jutted over the sidewalks on either side of the road. They seemed to strain on their cast iron supports and were filled to overflowing with drunken young people.

Brightly colored beaded necklaces sailed through the air from above and below, and more than a few girls lifted their blouses to afford the passersby a glimpse of bare flesh in exchange for a tossed plastic prize. The girls with the most necklaces undoubtedly flashed their wares more than the others. Doctor was amused, but he did not join in on their bawdy revelry.

Walking along Bourbon Street behind Doctor, Jim paid no heed to the peep shows. Instead, he kept a close eye on the buxom blond woman up ahead who wore a sequined and feathered fascinator. She pretended to stumble and lunged forward. Doctor caught her before she fell and held her steady with a firm grip on her shoulder. Soon the two were engaged in a lively conversation. Her colorful feathers bobbed and quivered as her tinkling laughter erupted. Doctor echoed her merriment in a booming baritone.

When the woman tried to link her arm in his, however, Doctor abruptly pulled back out of her grasp. He bypassed the barrier and commissioned the first in a line of parked taxis on the cross street, leaving the blond in the middle of Bourbon Street with her lips pouting beneath the gaudy party hat.

Smart move, thought Jim, relieved that Doctor was intuitive enough to sense the danger in the seemingly chance encounter. Doctor was the woman's target, as well, but for a different reason. Jim was ever aware of her presence in all the places he had already followed Doctor. He had surmised the woman's intent, but he did not know her name, so he referred to her as "*Covetress.*" She followed the money, and Jim knew she was dangerous.

Throwing his arm out, Jim appeared to the next taxi driver and followed Doctor, knowing that, although *Covetress* was still behind them on the street, she would inevitably show up at the next casino, in the next town, in the next state.

After a short drive, Doctor exited his cab, paid his fare, and strode to a recreational vehicle parked at the curb. He unlocked the door of the silver and black 1993 Winnebago Brave 31RQ. The brand new 31-foot fully outfitted luxury motorhome had been Doctor's traveling residence for the past six months, paid for in cash with some of his earlier winnings from Las Vegas.

Jim also exited his cab. Slipping in unseen before Doctor closed the door, he settled into the seat of one of the leather club chairs and prepared for the journey. His host had no idea he had taken on a passenger. Jim had, in fact, been Doctor's passenger for the entire time he had owned the RV. But Doctor would only be able to see him if Jim willed it, and Jim had no desire to be seen. Doctor pulled out into the street, and Jim went to sleep.

CHAPTER TWO
THE QUEST BEGINS

LIAHONA THISTLESEED'S HOUSE always seems to be the departure point for the Trackers Team's journeys. Today is no exception. At 7:00 in the morning, it is already hot and humid in Tallahassee, and the air conditioner is humming away. The Trackers and their family members mill around, giving the home the appearance of a family reunion with all ages of relatives from infants to teens to adults.

Gathered inside are Lee and Wren, who are in their mid-forties, and all the Thistleseed children: nearly 25-year-old Shine and her twin Cyrus, 20-year-old Jubal and his twin Selah, 17-year-old twins Deborah and Zipporah, Chenaniah, who celebrates his thirteenth birthday next month, and little Shelly, who is nine. The newest members of the Thistleseed family are Sali Mata and her brother Arfang, both pressed close to Bill.

The Lightfoot family members include 30-year-old Dane and his 28-year-old wife Raven, Raven's mother Robin Looking Bird, exactly one month younger than Wren, and the four-week-old baby boys, Perry and Buck. The other Lightfoot present is Dane's 19-year-old brother Noah, the charming and powerful remote viewer with a photographic memory. He is accompanied by his 18-year-old girlfriend, Maria Ramirez, a clairempath dream catcher who is in training as a Tracker.

The newly created Skysong family is small, but mighty, and consists of 31-year-old Graham Skysong and his bride of one month, Shinehah Thistleseed.

Usually, when the Trackers Team travels—either on land or sea or in their minds—they have a destination, or at least a perpetrator or missing person on whom to focus. Lee is normally the Tracker who maps out their destinations via poetic metaphor using his psychic remote viewing ability.

This time, everything is vastly different. They are to go at the whim of two revolving spindles within a strange open ball made of brass. Were it not for their deep and abiding faith, it would seem a madman's journey, but the Thistleseeds are dedicated and obedient followers of God's will. Lee, as the leader of the Trackers Team, sets the example for Dane and Graham, who will accompany him.

Wren, Raven, and Shinehah must trust their men. There have been other tracks, and all the members of the Team have been exposed to many types of danger. Tracking is not without risks. They all know this. But, sometimes, it is of little comfort when they face the absolute unknown. Therefore, each woman has packed her husband's bag with extra special care.

In the master bedroom, Wren Thistleseed bustles about, making sure she has included everything her spouse may possibly need on this unknown quest that began with the unearthing of the *Liahona*. His soft-sided suitcase contains clothing, pictures of the family, and his dog-eared scriptures.

In a side zippered compartment, Wren tucks away a special letter she stayed up late into the night writing, telling him of her deep and undying love and respect for him and praying for his success and safe return. She is thankful that Graham and Dane will accompany her soul mate. She trusts them with her husband's very life.

Raven Lightfoot stuffed Dane's duffle bag with suitable clothing for both hot and cold climates. Since his clairscent/clairalient smelling powers have finally returned with the renewed growth of his hair—hacked off by muggers in a track a little over a year ago—Dane has taken to wearing it pulled back into a long ponytail. Raven packed extra elastic bands for that purpose. She also stashed away some cleansing sage bundles to keep his olfactory senses clear, along with several packets of *"Fawn-tea."*

Dane's mother, Fawn, is a Seminole Cedar Woman—a healer gifted in medicinal arts with herbs and potions. Her special organic herbal blend tea saved Raven's life when she was poisoned by ecstasy-laced perfume. *It never hurts to have some on hand,* Raven thinks, stuffing more tea into the bag.

She has also included pictures—mostly of their sons Perry and Buck, who were born wrapped in each other's arms during an Arizona blizzard, beneath a spreading pine tree on a mountainside. Miracles, the both, and gifted with their own unique psychic gifts, even now they are alert and aware, fussing in their baby carriers on the hearth.

Shinehah, as a newlywed, has had little time to know Graham's ways as a husband; however, he has been a family friend for the past several years, and she has a unique understanding of him that the other wives do not share with their own husbands. She knows him as a big brother who uses his psychic clairaudient hearing and mimicry skills to entertain her brothers and sisters; as a mentor for her youngest brother, Kenny, whose psychic gifts as a medium, a channel, and a master of languages have recently awakened; as a loving son and nephew who saved his family in New Mexico by finding and defeating his father's murderer; as a kind and gentle partner and lover; and, soon, as a father himself, as evidenced by her expanding waistline.

They have only just returned from their honeymoon, and now he must leave her. They did not even have time to unpack his bag but only added a fleece hoodie in case he must go to a colder climate. It is a bittersweet parting, but Shine has a fierce conviction that he will be kept safe.

She removes her necklace—a turquoise pendant carved with the likeness of a young woman and strung on a rope of braided sinew—and places it around his neck. The necklace is special to the two of them. It is *Asdz Nádleehé* — Changing Woman. It represents Shine's new role as a wife and an expectant mother. It was given to Shine by an aged Navajo woman and was instrumental in the battle against the supernatural monsters that threatened their lives just weeks ago. Graham kisses the carving and pushes it inside his shirt. Then, he places his big hand on Shine's slightly protruding belly and brushes his lips against the top of her head. The child she carries will be called Natalie, and Graham vows he *will* return to her and her mother.

"He's here," Shelly calls from the foyer.

The familiar burgundy van driven by John Revell pulls up in the circular driveway. John steps out and adjusts his sunglasses against the glare of the morning sun. Shelly opens the door and waves at him, smiling broadly.

Lee, Dane, and Graham grab their bags and descend the steps, placing their luggage into the back of the vehicle. Then, they come back into the house, along with John, who greets everyone warmly.

"Folks, I don't know where we will be led, or what we will find, but I'm sure the Lord has a great purpose in this quest. Can we have a word of prayer?" he asks.

The whole of the household bow their heads, including

Graham, Robin, Raven, and Noah, who are not traditional churchgoers.

"Heavenly Father, we are thankful for the opportunity to do thy will and for this quest we are about to embark upon. We know not the reasons, nor the outcome, but we know the One who sends us. Let us be diligent, faithful, and successful, even as Lehi and his people were faithful in following the guidance of the *Liahona* in ancient times. Bless us with strength of purpose; enlighten us with the promptings of the Holy Spirit; lead, guide, and direct us to a fruitful conclusion of this quest; and keep us safe in the hollow of thy hands that we may return victorious. In the name of your most Holy Son, Jesus Christ. Amen," John prays.

At the conclusion of the prayer, many tears are shed as families embrace each other. Then, the four chosen men descend the steps, enter the van, and embark on the quest.

* * *

In Louisiana, amid the steamy heat of the morning, three men stood together on a public sidewalk on Canal Street, palms raised, their faces turned toward the sky. Though the streets were already beginning to fill with vehicle and foot traffic, not a soul noticed the men. As people walked by, they instinctively sidestepped the trio without knowing why they changed paths.

"Hallelujah! The journey is nigh," the youngest said, "I would go to the mountain to await their coming."

"Hallelujah! The travelers have begun the quest," the middle one said, "I would stay in the south until the chosen one moves onward."

"Hallelujah! The Compass shall show the way," the oldest said, "I would go to the north where the ancestors have long crossed over."

One by one, they embraced and kissed each other's cheeks, and then they trod away in different directions. Nobody questioned their behavior; nobody saw them at all.

* * *

Upon leaving Tallahassee, John and the Trackers decide to travel outside the populated areas before they try to use the *Liahona* compass. On the outskirts of the city, they come upon a rest stop that presents a semi-deserted grassy stretch near the back side. Pulling the van to the curb, they disembark and walk the short distance to the edge of the woods stretch that border the grass. Stepping just inside the cover of the trees, they stand in a square facing one another.

Lee removes the ball from the velveteen drawstring bag that Wren fashioned for it. Dane holds the bag while Lee positions the *Liahona* awkwardly in his cupped hands. They don't know what to expect, but everyone seems to stop breathing for a few seconds.

Then, the spindles inside the compass begin to rotate. They spin to the right, then to the left, and then to the right again. And then they stop moving. The outside of the ball is unchanged, but Lee sees writing appear inside the ball. It seems to be Hebrew, but it is not something Lee can read. He is immediately flustered. *Of what use is this compass if I cannot interpret the directions?* he thinks.

As though reading his mind, John Revell leans in closer, holds his breath, and peers down into the ball.

"North. Look, it directs us to go north," John says as he exhales. "We have to go north."

"How do you know that, John?" Lee asks.

"I…I don't know, exactly. I studied ancient languages in college. I can read Hebrew, and I can read some Aramaic and even some cuneiform. I assumed the writing might be one of those. I don't know why, but…but this looks to me like it's in plain old English!" John stammers.

"No. Way," Graham says.

"Yes way, I think," Dane says in disbelief.

"North. That can be a lot of ways," Lee says.

"North to the mountains," John says.

"What mountains?" Dane asks, "Lots of mountains in the north."

John squints at the compass. "Tennessee," he says.

"Dude. It can't say Tennessee. I can get behind 'north,' but specifically 'Tennessee?' Nah," Dane says.

"I don't know what to tell you," John says with a shrug. "I distinctly see the word 'Tennessee' inside that ball. It's written on the top spindle."

Dane and Graham look at Lee for confirmation. He stares back at them with a queasy expression on his face.

"Lee?" Graham prompts.

"I do not see the word 'Tennessee,' but there is definitely a word written on that spindle that was not there when I first looked into the top. If John sees 'Tennessee,' then I think it must be so. Sometimes we are not all meant to be witnesses to everything that presents itself," Lee admits.

"I've got an idea," Dane says. "Just hear me out. This is a tremendous leap of faith for us...not to mention Graham, who is not used to some of our peculiar LDS happenings. Just for the sake of clarity—not doubting you, John—but because we do what we do, let's let Lee do a bit of tracking each time after we look at the compass."

"That makes perfect sense to me, Dane. Then we can have confirmation of a direction. Just in case, you know," Graham says, ever the diplomat.

"I agree," John says.

"Do you?" Lee asks.

"Of course. I think it's the wise thing to do. Then we can be sure I'm really seeing what I think I'm seeing, and we're on the right track, so to speak," John says.

"Good deal!" Graham says. He reaches into his back pants pocket and withdraws two 3x5 notebooks with pencils stuck in the spirals.

"Dude, you came prepared, didn't you? Did Shine do

that for you?" Dane says.

"My wife is a wise woman, but these notebooks came courtesy of..." Graham says.

"Kenny!" Dane shouts, pumping his fist in the air.

"Bingo," Graham confirms.

"OK, John. Here's how it works. We're all going to sit down on the ground. Lee is going to go into a trance, and so will I. When he starts talking, you and Graham will write down everything...and I mean everything...he says. Then we'll wake up and decipher it. Got it?" Dane says, passing John a notebook and pencil.

John takes the offered notebook, closes his open mouth, and immediately sits down cross-legged. The others follow suit. Lee and Dane begin breathing deeply, and the track begins with Lee's long exhale.

"The elephant is tethered in the south, but it will soon tread to the north. It will climb the hills and disappear into the smoke. The creatures that ride the elephant move from wager to wager, gathering talents on the way. They will visit the hippos on the water; they will visit the rhinos on the land. They will gather the talents as they go, but the she-jackal follows close behind. The elephant will rest near the smoke for a time, but the Trackers shall get there first, for after a bit of rest, the elephant will travel again to another hunting ground. Beware, beware, the she-jackal is ever on its trail, and the Tracker must now come home," Lee says.

Lee shudders and seems to come awake. Dane sighs and wakes immediately afterward. Both men look at the other two who are already consulting their notes.

"That was the most bizarre thing I have ever witnessed," John admits.

"I'm with you there, John. I've never heard him use these animals before," Graham says.

"No, I mean the whole tracking thing. The sleeping trance, the talking, and then waking up. Why did Dane go to sleep, too? He didn't say anything," John says.

"We track as partners, John. One person takes a mental journey, and the other sends a mental signal—much like a beacon from a lighthouse on the shore. Dane's light gave my tracking mind a point on which to focus so I could return my mind to my body," Lee explains.

"Oh, that makes it abundantly clear," John laughs.

Dane scoots over and looks at Graham's notes.

"This was weird, Lee. Just weird," Graham says.

"Are you kidding me? Weird isn't the half of it," Dane says. "Lee, this is going to be a doozy of a trip!"

"All right, boys. I get it. It was a bit different. Shall we decipher it while it is yet fresh?" Lee prompts.

"Well, you've never used an elephant before, so I have to assume it's bigger than a regular car or truck. My guess is a bus or a motorhome," Graham says.

"Yep. I think so, too. Probably an RV, though. An

elephant would be black or grey, don't ya think? I think bus, and I see...well...yellow. Was it yellow?" Dane says.

"He didn't say, Dane, but I'm going with RV, also. And it does go north, like John said. Climbs the hills and disappears into the smoke. Could there be a fire?" Graham says.

"I may be wrong, but I'm thinking maybe that means the Smoky Mountains. And that's definitely in Tennessee," John says.

"OK. One point for you. Tennessee, it is," Dane says.

"But what about hippos on water; rhinos on land? That is certainly not Tennessee," Lee says.

"Good point, Lee. They're going other places, but they'll eventually end up in the Smoky Mountains. Hippos and Rhinos? Really big buildings, maybe," Graham says.

"Ah, yes. I concur," Lee says nodding.

"What about this part: 'move from wager to wager, gathering talents on the way.' What's that?" Dane asks.

"I know! A wager is a bet. And talents, in ancient times, referred to money instead of abilities. So, where do you bet money?" John prompts.

"Betting is most often done in casinos, of course," Lee says. "They must be going from casino to casino. They are gamblers traveling in a motorhome."

"What's this about a she-jackal that's following them?" Dane asks.

"A predator who means to rob them and do them harm.

Jackals are notoriously vicious, so this woman—gotta be a woman if it's a she—must be really dangerous," Graham says.

"Well, if you fellows are in agreement, can we get on the road to Tennessee before they go to the happy hunting ground?" John asks, rising and casually brushing off his pants.

Lee looks at him carefully. Though the man tried hard to mask his feelings, his tone of voice and his clenching jaws alarm Lee. The comment about "the happy hunting ground" seems off-base. Graham's notes read "*another* hunting ground," not "*happy* hunting ground." In all his repertoire of Native American Indian stories, the happy hunting ground is a place of death, like a burial ground. Something is very wrong, and John Revell has knowledge of it. This journey may pose more danger than what they first anticipated. Lee decides he will have to keep a close eye and ear on his friend.

The Trackers get up and follow John to the van, now excited that they have a real destination and are able to use their familiar tracking skills to pinpoint it. Only Lee seems to have noticed the oddness about John's declaration, but he keeps it to himself so as not to influence the others. However, it bears remembering and, quite probably, a private call to Chenaniah later to see what information his psychic link Luna can give them.

CHAPTER THREE
<u>OPRYLAND HOTEL</u>

DANE CLUCKS HIS TONGUE appreciatively when he enters the room he and Graham will share. The two men smile and high-five each other as they take in the sumptuous décor. This room may not be the Presidential Suite, but it is significantly more opulent than one in which either of them has ever stayed. Upon arriving in Tennessee, John insisted they register at the Opryland Hotel in Nashville before traveling farther up into the Smoky Mountains.

"Not bad," Graham observes, dropping his bag on one overstuffed queen-sized bed.

"Not bad? I'd say a whole heap better than 'not bad,' dude," Dane says. He drops his duffle bag on the floor and propels himself backwards, landing heavily onto the other queen-sized bed and sinking deep into the plush duvet.

A knock on the adjoining French doors commands their attention. Opening the glass-paneled doors inward, Graham allows Lee to enter the room while immediately thrusting his head into the larger suite from which Lee emerged. He takes in its furnishings, which include a gleaming kitchenette, six-chair mahogany dinette set, two brocade high-backed reading chairs, and a matching settee.

By contrast, the attached bedroom he and Dane share is rather plain, but it still far exceeds their expectations. He emits an appreciatory whistle and is greeted with the amused face of John Revell coming from the suite's master bathroom.

"Is your room satisfactory, Graham?" John asks.

"Oh, yeah. It's very satisfactory. Yours?" Graham says.

"Quite," John chuckles.

"Graham, come in here, please," Lee says, "and close the door. Let John get settled."

Graham grins and waves awkwardly at John, and then he gingerly closes the doors and pulls out the Queen Anne style chair from his own room's writing desk on which to sit. Dane remains spread-eagled on the bed, hands behind his head.

"What's the news, Hona?" Dane asks.

"I have no news, but I wanted to talk with the two of you before we go any further. I would like to know what impressions you have received thus far," Lee whispers.

"Impressions...you mean, like psychic impressions?" Graham asks, speaking sotto voce to match Lee's soft voice.

"Well, yes and no. I am curious as to any of your impressions—psychic or non. Specifically, how do you feel about this quest? We have very little information on which to base anything. I am not even sure whom or what we should be tracking, at this point," Lee says.

"I agree, Lee. I like John Revell. He seems like a stand-up guy, but he is rather cryptic. He has only released the barest details of his involvement, yet he seems to be taking the lead about where we go," Graham says.

"Yeah, I caught that. It's like he's in charge...but I thought this was your gig, Hona. I mean, you found the compass, you're the one Kenny said had to make the journey. We're just tagalongs, kindof. And how's he paying for things? You know, like this two-room suite in this fancy hotel, which is really, really nice, by the way, but I woulda been fine with Motel 6," Dane whispers.

"Me, too. And no offense, but I'm pretty much out in left field in this group. You three guys have your church stuff to fall back on. I'm not of your faith, so I don't know how much I can contribute. That old compass doesn't even move when I hold it," Graham says, hunching his brawny shoulders.

"Graham, you are extremely important. Just because we do not hold the same religious views does not mean your opinions are not of value. Chenaniah said you were to be part of this, and my son—young and inexperienced as he is—seems to have a unique perspective and understanding of all things

Trackers. I have always thought of you as my son, even before you were married to my daughter. That the *Liahona* does not move in your hands is of no concern to me. *I* need you, Graham. *I* do," Lee says.

Graham shuffles his big feet, embarrassed and touched by his father-in-law's words. "OK. I'm good," he mumbles.

"Is there a plan of any sort?" Dane asks.

At that moment, they hear a knock on the room's front door. Rising to answer it, Graham is startled to see John on the indoor balcony that circles the huge downstairs common area. He has showered and changed into clean shirt and trousers.

"Hello, everyone. I just wanted to let you guys know that I'm going downstairs to the Atrium to get something cold to drink and to stretch my legs for a bit. Got your key card, Lee?" John says.

"Oh, yes. It is in my pocket here," Lee responds.

"Good. I won't be long. Just taking a stroll. I'll be back before dinner, say about 6:00? That work for y'all? John says.

"That will be just fine," Lee says. "It will give us all time to rest and get cleaned up. Thank you, John."

John smiles and waves before pulling the door closed.

Nobody says anything for several minutes. Each is absorbed in thought. Then, as though emerging from a fog, Lee regards the others. "Going to get a shower. Change my clothes. And maybe take a nap. Be back here by 6:00," he mutters, disappearing through the adjoining French doors.

35

Graham and Dane exchange puzzled looks.

"Wow. He's kindof out of it, right now. He didn't even use complete sentences, and I think I counted at least two contractions. Totally out of character for Lee," Dane says.

"I noticed that, Dane. He's clearly engaged in some kind of mental dilemma," Graham agrees.

"Gray, what's happening here?" Dane asks.

"I don't know, buddy, but I'm thinking we better clean up and do some reconnaissance before Lee comes back over. Something's really weird...well, weirder than usual...about all this," Graham says.

"Righto," Dane replies. He jumps up from the bed and bounds into the bathroom. After a few minutes of splashing water and toilet flushing, he emerges with damp hair and a toothbrush clamped between his teeth.

"Are you done already?" Graham asks.

"Sure," Dane responds. "Doesn't take long to wash the necessary parts. Hurry up. I'm anxious to do some spying."

Graham takes the hint, and though his bathroom time is barely seconds longer, he emerges clean and ready to go. The two men exit their room and begin a leisurely meandering stroll around the balcony promenade that overlooks the plant-filled Atrium of the Opryland Hotel, looking for John Revell.

*　*　*

"Shemnon reports that the woman is still in pursuit," the man told John. "They have encountered her in three different locations."

John regarded his tablemate solemnly, nodding his head upon hearing the news.

Though roughly the same age as John Revell—thirty-something to forty-something—the man was possessed of a maturity well beyond his chronological age. He was good-looking, medium in stature, dusky skinned, with soft black hair that covered his head in naturally curling waves and formed tiny ringlets above his ears. His small, dark brown eyes were flecked with unusual silver striations around the irises, as though reflecting flashing lights.

The man's given name was Mathoni—a word, in Hebrew, which meant "my gift." But to his friends and acquaintances in America, he was known as Matt Tonai. His ancestral heritage was distinctive: a Jaredite, his people originated during the time when the Tower of Babel was destroyed and man's language was confounded. Most of his tribesmen were Israelite descendants of Joseph, the boy whose brothers sold him into slavery in Egypt, where he eventually became a ruler.

John frowned as he considered the news. "Is he well?" he asked, his voice cracking just a little.

"Apparently, he is quite well...and still winning at every gaming place in which he stops," Matt said.

John shook his head. "To have such a healing gift and to waste his time in monetary pursuits, I cannot understand what happened," he said.

"It is not your fault, John. We realize that men have free agency to choose their actions. That is God's will, after all. We can only do so much to guide them. In the end, a man must make his own way. For now, we can only do our best to intervene indirectly," Matt said.

"I know, my friend. I get weary with the worry, though," he admitted.

"Don't we all?" Matt agreed. "I am worried about my loved ones, too."

"Yes, Mathoni. I know what the consequences are to your family as well if we are not successful," John consoled.

Matt's eyes misted momentarily. "I know you do," he said. "You have been my friend and confidant for a long time."

"As I will continue to be," John said, placing his hand on his friend's shoulder.

"I have faith we will triumph, John," Matt said.

"Tell me. If the woman gets too close, if she threatens to harm him, can Shemnon stop her?" John asked.

"Most assuredly, and he will be victorious. The Doctor is too important for us to let his destiny be compromised. Though they are his own choices he makes, it is not against the Father's will for us to keep him safe. The very course of the future rests on this quest. Is the Compass equal to the task?" Matt asked tentatively.

"Yes. I believe so. The man is faithful, and the *Liahona*

works within his hands," John confirmed.

"And the other two?" Matt asked.

"Their gifts will present themselves at the proper time. They are young and brash, but their hearts are pure. I feel we can trust them to choose the right course of action," John said.

"Very well," Matt said. Glancing upward, he switched seamlessly from English to another language entirely. "I'm glad you have faith in them. Perhaps now is the time to turn and wave. They are directly above us on the balcony."

John's eyes opened wide, but he kept his body still, resisting the urge to look up.

"Let us keep up this charade and tarry a while longer, my friend. Stand and bid me farewell, and I will introduce you this evening as our dinner guest and traveling companion," John replied, in the same language.

Then, ignoring the two Trackers peeking through the foliage a few floors above them, the two men shook hands and moved in different directions. John made his way back to the hotel room slowly to give the two spies time to beat him there.

* * *

Dane and Graham barely make it through the door of their room when they hear Lee knocking on the window of the French doors. Dane swings the doors open and admits Lee, who regards him quizzically.

"It is nearly 6:00, Dane. Are you not ready?" he says.

"Sure, I'm ready, Hona. Even brushed my teeth. Just

39

gotta pull my hair back," Dane says.

"Then, why are you so sweaty...and smelly?" Lee observes, nose wrinkling.

"It's hot here...and...uh...Graham won't let me use his aftershave," Dane says.

Graham's eyes and mouth open wide. As a clairalient with exceptional powers of smell, Dane *never* wears aftershave or cologne because it interferes with his ability to detect scents. Graham is afraid Lee will see through Dane's fabricated explanation. Glancing at his friend, he notices a bead of sweat coursing down the side of his face. Dane also realizes the faux pas he has made. Lying does not come easily to either of them.

"Graham, please share," Lee huffs.

"Oh, sorry, sorry. It's just down here in my bag. Here ya go, Dane. Have all you want." Graham speaks quickly and a bit too loudly as he tosses the bottle across the bed.

Dane douses himself with Graham's Brut aftershave. When he finishes, he holds his arms out, grinning at Lee like a lunatic. "Ta da," he sings.

Lee shakes his head and grimaces, sighing heavily.

"What can I say, Lee. The boy has no couth." Graham attempts to laugh.

A knock at the outer door saves them from any further explanation. John enters the room, sniffs the overpowering fragrance of the Brut, and smiles knowingly.

"Hello, guys! The Atrium is just beautiful and so

refreshing after that long drive. You will really enjoy it. I have arranged for us to have a table near the cascading indoor waterfall. Are you ready? I'm starving!" John says.

The Trackers exit the room with sounds of agreement.

"Oh, and I have a wonderful surprise! I happened to come upon an old friend of mine from college. His name is Matt Tonai, and not only will he be joining us for dinner, he's going to travel with us for a while. Isn't that great?" John says.

"That is delightful, John," Lee says, walking beside John on the balcony. "Do you not agree, boys?"

Falling into step behind them, Dane and Graham look at each other, blinking rapidly. "Oh, yeah, that's great. Uh-huh. Good news. Sure thing," they mumble.

CHAPTER FOUR
<u>BILOXI, MS</u>

"WINNER, WINNER, CHICKEN DINNER!" the man beside the Doctor shouted when the slot machine began spitting out silver dollars. Doctor gave a pained grin. He held his buckets beneath the coin return and collected the change until the machine stopped spitting it out. He left his seat then and cashed in, stuffing $1,200 in hundred-dollar bills into his pants pocket. He stood still a moment, leveling his head in the side to side motion he used when sensing a machine about to turn over. *Nothing. They've all gone dark.*

Shrugging, Doctor bid farewell to the *Isle of Caprice* casino. He was officially played out in Mississippi. He had previously won cash at the two riverboat casinos—*Grand Casinos* and *Casino Magic*. His earnings on those boats was well over $6,000. Thereafter, he made his way to the shore.

Though Mississippi had made it legal to gamble aboard cruise ships in 1989, it was not until the state legislature passed the Mississippi Gaming Control Act in 1990 that dockside gambling was approved. The *Isle of Caprice* was one of three land-based casinos which had opened in 1992. Doctor had played them all, but he found the *Isle of Caprice* rather stingy. The machines were tight, and the payouts were small.

It was time to move on. Outside on the boardwalk, breathing in the salty air, he thought back to the casinos from which he had recently come. There had been many, and he had won a considerable amount of money, allowing him to operate exclusively by cash.

He had gambled thus far in three states in the U.S. Naturally, Nevada provided the most variety. He had hit the strip first, but he found the crowds distracting. There were just too many people and too much bright light for him to focus on the impressions that invariably led him to winning machines. And, of course, there was always the chance he would be recognized. Las Vegas had a lot of paparazzi, and his was a recognizable face. Having received a notable award at one of the grandest hotels in the "City of Lights" for his professional accomplishments, which led to quite a bit of publicity, he preferred to stay out of the limelight and under the radar, lest anyone learn his whereabouts. So, he stuck to out-of-the-way places in the state like Carson City, Truckee, Sparks, Fernley, and Winnemucca.

After that, he made his way to the "Lone Star" state and gambled aboard the *Star of Texas* casino cruise that operated out of the Port of Galveston. He won nearly $4,000 on that cruise before it returned to port. Next was the "Big Easy."

He particularly liked the Louisiana casinos. The ambiance of the *Star Casino* and the *Casino Rock Island* were charming, the slots were loosie-goosie, and the sights and sounds of "Nawlins" amused him. *Those were good pickings, cher,* he thought, smiling at the term of endearment that was used for both men and women. Doctor especially loved the mélange of smells from spicy Cajun cooking in boardwalk bistros and the taste of sweet, powdered sugar beignets with strong, hot coffee.

It was hard to believe that just a few short months had passed since Doctor whetted his appetite in his first casino visit in Freeport, Bahamas. The *Princess Casino* was part of a sprawling resort owned by Merv Griffin on 80 tropical acres surrounded by the glorious translucent blue and green waters of the Caribbean, with 21 tennis courts, a world-class 18-hole golf course, four swimming pools, and 35 restaurants and bars.

Having never gambled before, he was hypnotized by the flashing lights, the clanging bells, and the undulating tide of customers as they tried their luck on machines and at tables with coins, cards, and chips. The colleagues who introduced him to this experience never realized what a gateway drug it would become for him.

Doctor was cautious at first. Even though he had more than enough resources at his disposal, he bet only a few dollars here and there. He added up playing cards to get as close as he could to the magical number of 21 without going over. He threw red plastic cubes toward the end of a green, felt-covered table, hoping not to "crap out" if the white dots on the dice equaled two or seven. He placed chips on red or black numbered squares and watched as a man spun a huge clacking wheel to see what number eventually stopped under the pointer. He sat at round tables with other people, holding and trading in cards to make a hand of five cards that were at least three of the same kind, but aiming for five numbers in sequence, a combination of two plus three of a kind, or four of the same number or picture of royalty.

He grew tired of counting numbers, and leaving his colleagues to the tables, he wandered over to the rows of small metal contraptions. Doctor saw people sitting on vinyl-padded stools before various rectangular machines, feeding pennies, nickels, dimes, quarters, and even silver dollars into vertical coin slots and pulling levers attached to the right side of the apparatuses. He leveled his head left and right looking at the rows upon rows of people pulling the handles.

The players were in various trance-like states, with blank staring eyes, unattended cigarettes going to ash, and beaded sweat on their upper lips, clutching plastic buckets of change that they kept feeding into the coin slots. He was fascinated. The physician and scholar within himself thought, *there's a research paper in this phenomenon. I need to investigate further.* And so, he chose a seat at a vacant machine that seemed brighter than the others on the row. Reaching into his pocket, he withdrew a quarter and inserted it into the coin slot. Grasping the lever, he pulled it toward himself, noting the satisfying feel of the metal in his grip as it hit its stopper. He released the lever, and it sprang back to its starting position.

Doctor watched as pictures of colored fruit spun in three vertical columns. The first column stopped on a picture of a purple plum, then the second column, and finally the third. Three plums were side by side beneath a horizontal line drawn on the machine's front window. Immediately, bells began to clang, and quarters were ejected into a large opening beneath the window. He quickly grabbed a left-behind bucket beside the contraption and scooped the quarters into it. He had won $8.50. Not a bad return for an investment of 25 cents.

He put another quarter into the slot, noticing idly that the machine seemed less bright than it did when he first sat down. After pulling the lever and watching the spinning fruit, the result was three mismatched shapes: an orange, a plum, a lemon. No coins dropped into the opening. He tried again and got another result: a lemon, an orange, and a number seven.

Bored, he vacated his seat and walked around, his bucket of quarters jangling, until he saw another machine that seemed noticeably bright, shiny, and clean. He perched himself on the stool.

"That one's a dud," the balding man beside him said.

"How do you know that?" Doctor asked.

The man jerked a thumb over his shoulder. "That old lady's been feeding that one-armed bandit for over an hour. Nothing. But, hey, have at it," he said.

Doctor glanced at the machine again. *One-armed bandit. Quaint name,* he thought. He looked over at the man's machine. It was exactly the same model as his, but it seemed old, dirty, dull. By contrast, Doctor's bandit seemed to nearly glow. He fished in his bucket and withdrew five quarters. Apparently, one could insert multiple coins for a larger return. He fed his bandit and pulled its arm.

As before, the rows and columns spun, creating a rainbow of colors before his eyes. The spinning slowed, and the pictures dropped into their places behind the horizonal line: number seven, number seven, number seven.

Whereas the first machine gave a modest one-pitch *ding-ding-ding-ding-ding*, this machine now emitted a louder, non-ending trio of tones. Lights atop the bandit flashed red, and coins began gushing from its mouth. They filled the bucket entirely, as well as two other buckets offered by people pressing in around him. The nearby regulars gave various sounds of approval, awe, and disgruntlement.

An attendant appeared, dressed in a gilt vest and black bowtie. He moved Doctor aside and inserted a key into the top of the machine, which immediately silenced the clanging and stopped the revolving light. As Doctor followed the attendant to the payout booth, he glanced back at the slot machine and was surprised to see that it no longer glowed. It was as dark as an unlit lamp.

Doctor's winnings from that one pull of the lever were a whopping $3,885.75. He took the payout in a combination of large and small bills, plus three quarters. As he met up with his congratulatory friends at the door, he took one more look back at the casino. He could see a mixture of bright and dull slot machines all along the aisles, and he instinctively understood: the bright ones paid, and the dull ones didn't.

Doctor went on to garner his largest winnings at the *Paradise Island Resort* in its 30,000 square-foot world class casino. After more success at the *Carnival Crystal Palace*, a resort and casino on Cable Beach near Nassau, and the *Lucayan Beach Casino* on Grand Bahama Island, he hopped a flight back to America, paying for his ticket in cash.

"Winner, winner, chicken dinner? Who says that?" he mused aloud. He didn't hear the woman approach until she spoke behind him.

"Are you looking for another game, honey?" she asked.

Doctor turned to see a beautiful woman as sultry as the night air. She was exotic: a petite Asian with dark, almond-shaped eyes and cherry-red lips fixed in a pout. A crimson satin headband was tied behind her bangs and around her glossy, chin-length black hair. Her scarlet dress, if it could be called a dress instead of a slip, fit snugly and showed every curve. She licked her lips and tossed her hair provocatively, regarding him slyly beneath thick lashes.

"Ah, hello. Well, I think I have been to all the casinos here," he said politely.

"I was speaking of *ishtaboli*. Would you like to place a little wager on some Indian stickball?" she asked.

"Come again? Stickball?" Doctor said.

"It's *highly* competitive and sometimes *brutal*." She breathed heavily, "two teams score points by hurling a ball against the opposite goal post. They use special, hard sticks. No helmets. No padding. High stakes. Big wins."

Doctor noticed the rising color in her cheeks and the throbbing pulse in her neck when she described the game. Alluring as she was, she was also alarming. She seemed almost predatory. He took a step back, and she stepped forward. He stepped to the side, and she parried. He began to perspire.

"I love watching the Indians compete. They're so *primal*. Choctaw, Chickasaw, Cherokee, Creek," she intoned, her voice taking on a rhythmic quality. "Sometimes it's a bloodbath." She nearly panted, not taking her eyes from his.

"I don't think so. I...I'm...I'm meeting someone. I...just...I...I've got to go," he stammered.

"No, you're not," she countered. "You're all alone. I saw you in there at the slots. Come on, honey. What've you got

49

to lose?" She flicked her tongue around her lips.

"No, really. I have a...a...friend who's..." he gulped. He was having a difficult time controlling his breathing.

She moved closer, and he could smell her perfume. It seemed familiar. His mind was addled. He was two full heads taller than the woman, but he was afraid.

Suddenly, a stranger appeared between them. He was carrying a casino bucket filled with nickels. The man stumbled, and in doing so, he upended the bucket. The coins cascaded onto the walkway between the predator and the prey. Their eye contact was broken, and Doctor turned and sprinted toward the parking area. The woman snapped her head around toward the intruder.

"You idiot! How dare you..." she snarled, no longer beautiful, but almost beastly.

There was no other person on the walk. The owner of the nickel bucket was nowhere to be seen.

The woman drew her hands into fists and shook from head to toe. She cursed and raised her head, letting out a guttural vocalization akin to a wild animal, and then she began striding down the walkway.

By the time she reached the parking lot, the silver and black Winnebago Brave was no longer there. She howled in fury and beat her fists on a nearby Ford sedan, leaving deep dents in the hood.

Doctor did not witness her tirade. He had already

turned onto the interstate. Something the woman said left an impression on him. Indian gaming. He was certainly not interested in stickball, but many tribes—such as the Seminole in Florida and the Cherokee in Georgia—operated casinos, and most of them had a preponderance of slot machines. Florida, being his home state, was completely out of the question. He considered Georgia, but ultimately decided to go north and get out of the heat.

New York state, that's the ticket, he decided. He pulled to the side of the road and consulted his Rand McNally Road Atlas. After mapping out his route, he pulled back onto the interstate and set off towards the northeast.

Jim sat beside Doctor in the passenger's captain chair. He was unseen, unspeaking, unknown, and the incident had left him unnerved. Next time, he would be better prepared. *Note to self,* he thought, *keep a bucket of coins handy.*

CHAPTER FIVE

LEHI's LIAHONA

AFTER A DELICIOUS DINNER in the coolness of the Atrium beside the churning indoor waterfall, the five men finish up their desserts and agree on a time to meet in the morning to resume their trip. Matt Tonai returns to his room. John and the Trackers assemble up in Lee's room to consult the *Liahona* for guidance on tomorrow's route.

"But we just got to Tennessee," Dane says, "and now the compass is saying 'Mississippi'?"

"Well, not exactly. There are four words: 'Nevada, Texas, Louisiana, Mississippi.' They keep appearing and disappearing on the spindles. It doesn't stop on any one word," John says. His exasperation is palpable.

"He is right," Lee confirms, "I cannot read them, but I can tell that each one is a different word, and they are, indeed, changing."

"What can that mean?" Graham asks.

"I interpret it to mean one of two things: Go to *all* those places or *do not* go to *any* of those places," Lee says.

"Wow, that's helpful, Lee. I wish *I* had thought of it," Dane sneers.

"Don't be such a doofus, Dane. None of us really understands this thing. It shows cardinal directions, and then it shows place names. It doesn't say, 'go here' or 'go there.' Interpreting it is really hit or miss, at this point," Graham says.

"Sorry. Missing my wife and sons," Dane explains.

"I completely understand. Same here," Graham says.

"In a way, what you say is true, Graham. I can only tell you what I read, But, beyond that, we're just working on the fly," John says.

"I have a strong feeling that the Liahona is showing us places that have already been visited," Lee says.

"Mmm. Maybe. You can draw a travel path through Texas, Louisiana, and Mississippi if you shoot down from Nevada and travel along the Gulf Coast. My opinion is that the next place you'd go is Florida, though—not Tennessee," Graham suggests.

"Yeah, Tennessee is a bit random, don't you think?" Dane agrees.

"Yes, but when Lee was tracking, he definitely related about smoke in the mountains. That is most assuredly not

Florida," John says.

"Gotta point there, John," Dane says.

"That is correct. John read 'Tennessee,' and we verified it when I tracked. We are where we are supposed to be at this time," Lee says.

The four men are sitting in the dinette chairs around the mahogany table. Lee places the compass in the center of the table, where it lies dormant. He sits back in his chair and stares at the ceiling, deep in thought. He is weary and frustrated at this turn of events.

Making a decisive move, Dane reaches into his back pocket and pulls out his pager. He sets it on the table beside the *Liahona* and leans forward, arms laid flat on the wooden surface, and fixes Lee with a stare.

"What?" Lee asks.

"We need some help, Hona. We *are* a team, you know, so let's use the Team," Dane says.

"I agree with Dane, Lee. Let's call Noah and get him to go take a look," Graham suggests.

"I had planned to speak with Chenaniah when I call Wren tonight," Lee says, glancing askance at John.

"Kenny's good, yeah. Maybe Luna has some insight. And maybe Raven can draw these guys...and even the jackal. *That* would be helpful," Dane says.

John sits quietly listening to the exchange. He is clearly uncomfortable, and Lee notices.

"John, what do you think?" Lee prompts.

"Well, I guess so. Um, you know your team, but do you think that's really what we need to do instead of following the *Liahona*?" he responds.

"Dane? Graham?" Lee says. He looks at each of them in turn, his eyebrows pushing up wrinkles in his forehead. He is fairly certain they have the same doubts he feels about their traveling companion. Graham takes the cue.

"This is what I think. We need to know *who* we're tracking, for one thing," he says. He pauses a moment, and then he looks directly at John. "And we need to have a little more information from *you*, John Revell."

"Fellas, I don't have any information to give you," John says, holding up his hands.

"Really? Who is this person...this doctor? Who is the woman who's after him? And what language were you speaking today with your friend?" Graham demands.

John sits blinking, but he makes no response. Lee sits up in his chair and looks from face to face at the men around the table.

"Graham? Dane? John? Let us lay all our cards on the table, so to speak. I need some explanation," he says.

"Earlier, before we left for dinner, Graham and I were walking on the balcony, and we saw John downstairs talking with this Matt guy, so we, uh, we..." Dane says.

"Dane just watched, Lee. *I'm* the one who listened. I

55

couldn't help it. I heard them discussing a doctor and a woman, in English and a foreign language," Graham admits.

"I am sorry, John, but you have to understand that these men are used to taking matters into their own hands. Graham is a clairaudient, and he hears beyond a normal person's ability to hear. He can even hear a whisper from across a crowded room. Dane is a clairscent, also called a clairalient, and he has an enhanced ability to detect smells." He looks sternly at Dane. "...which does him no good in this situation, does it, when you insist on compromising your ability with scented aftershave? I am not happy about them spying on you, but they do have a point. We need to know what we are dealing with in this quest. You seem to know more than you have let on. Perhaps you will share with us now?" Lee says.

John hangs his head, mulling over his answer. In a few moments, he takes a deep breath and looks around at his companions at the table.

"All right. I *do* know who we're following. It's a man I am acquainted with. He's a doctor. In fact, he's a very skilled surgeon. His name is Jackson Fisher," John says.

"And, we're following him why?" Dane asks.

"Well, several months ago, Dr. Fisher was a guest speaker at a medical conference in the Bahamas. On the last day of the conference, he went missing from the venue. He didn't attend any of the meetings, and he checked out of his room at the hotel. That, in and of itself, was not terribly surprising. He's been prone to leaving early to get back to his patients. The problem is, he *didn't* come back to America right away, nor did he check on his patients, and nobody has heard from him other than a letter stating that he was taking a sabbatical for an undetermined length of time," John relates.

"That's odd, yes. What makes this particular doctor so special?" Graham asks.

"Dr. Fisher is the only man, the only surgeon around who can perform some very particular, delicate procedures here in the United States. In 1992, Dr. Fisher was working in conjunction with the International Federation of Gynecology and Obstetrics. He published a revolutionary statement this year, in 1993, with the World Health Organization that led to an intensive investigation by their highest authority, the World Health Assembly. I told you that Dr. Fisher was the keynote speaker at that conference. He was presenting a paper on his findings that has world-wide significance," John says.

At the words "gynecology" and "obstetrics," a shiver runs down Graham's spine. *Is Shine all right?* he wonders. Although they are newlyweds of a little over a month, his wife became pregnant on their wedding night, and he worries about her condition constantly.

"Wow. Sounds like he's pretty important," Dane says.

"Very important," Johns acknowledges.

"What is his surgical specialty?" Lee asks.

"He's a plastic surgeon. He does reparative work of a

very specialized nature—body defacement, severe burns, facial deformities, disfiguring injuries, mutilations," John replies.

"OK. So, you're trying to find this famous plastic surgeon who is AWOL. Same question: Why?" Dane asks.

"There are some patients that require his skills, and these are very important patients," John says.

"Are they wealthy or something?" Graham asks.

John shakes his head slowly from side to side. "No, no. They are certainly not wealthy. At least one is indigent, in fact. He is a John Doe who was gravely injured and has been lying in a continuous unconscious state for a few years, and another is a young immigrant woman who has absolutely nothing to her name, but it's critical that we find Dr. Fisher. He's the only one who can help them and many others," he says.

"Huh! What makes them so important?" Dane asks.

John looks up and gives a tiny smile. "The Lord says they're important, Dane, if not now, then in the future in some way. That's why the *Liahona* is leading us to Dr. Fisher," John says with a shrug.

"Lee? What's your take on this?" Graham asks.

Lee frowns, and then he purses his lips and raises his eyebrows. "I trust John Revell. I have known him for some time, and I know him to be a worthy, honorable man. But, John, why did you not tell us this from the start instead of keeping such a secret? Did you not think we had a right to know? We have all left our families and our jobs to make this

58

quest," Lee says in a calm, but firm voice.

"Lee, I'm sorry, but I had to see for myself if you were the right man. The ancient *Liahona* works by faith, just as it did in the time of Lehi. It is only by faith that it will show the direction we must go. If I had told you in the beginning, would you have been operating on faith...or would you have been leaning to your own understanding?" John asks.

Now Lee hangs his head. He remembers what his son told him just a couple of days ago: *"If they didn't have faith, the Liahona didn't work. The people didn't exercise their faith and diligence, and they tarried in in the wilderness because of their transgressions."*

"You are right, John. I would have tried to impose my own knowledge and will on the compass. But do you think it will yet work for me?" Lee says.

"Do you still have faith?" John asks.

"I do," Lee says.

"Then it will work," Johns confirms with a smile.

"Time out," Graham says. "Maybe this is a good time for you guys to explain to me about this *Liahona* compass."

"I am delighted you asked, Graham," Lee says.

"Oh, way to go, dude. Here comes story time." Dane shakes his head, gets up, and plops down in a padded reading chair with his leg hanging over the arm.

As a history professor at Florida State University, Lee Thistleseed is known for his vast repertoire of stories, which he loves to relate to captive audiences. Lee sits up straighter in his chair and begins his recitation.

"In ancient days there was a righteous Israelite named Lehi, who was a prophet. He and his family fled into the wilderness from Jerusalem after evil men sought to destroy them. One morning, Lehi opened the door of his tent, and on the ground, he found a round brass ball of curious workmanship. Inside the ball were two spindles, one of which indicated the direction that his party should travel.

"In Lehi's language it was called a *Liahona*, which was the word for a compass. However, the *Liahona* differed from a modern-day magnetic compass in that it only worked if Lehi and his family were righteous and exerted the proper faith. In return for this faithfulness, the spindles pointed directionally, and the compass also delivered written instructions on the spindles and sometimes on the outside of the ball itself.

"Throughout time, Lehi and his family exercised their faith, even when the ball revealed that they would have to make a dangerous ocean voyage. They relied on the *Liahona* to bring them across the sea to the new world on the North American continent and to guide them to a land which the Lord had prepared for them.

"There was a time during the ocean crossing, however, that some of Lehi's sons rebelled against their father. When they did, the *Liahona* ceased to function, due to their loss of faith in God's commandments. When their faith and diligence were restored, the *Liahona* again gave them direction, and they were able to make it to America.

"After he became very elderly, Lehi passed the *Liahona* down to his righteous son Nephi, who was also a prophet. From generation to generation, the *Liahona* was passed down from father to son, through Mosiah and Benjamin, until it reached Moroni, the last Nephite prophet.

"In the fifth century A.D., Moroni buried the *Liahona* in a hill along with the historical records written on plates of gold that we call the Book of Mormon—named after the prophet Mormon who compiled the plates. In 1823, the prophet Joseph Smith was told by revelation where these sacred items were hidden. In the Book of Mormon, we learn in the chapter written by the prophet Alma more about the *Liahona*.

"Speaking to his son, Helaman, Alma explains that the *Liahona* was prepared and created by the Lord himself to show our forefathers the course of righteousness. It worked for them according to their faith in God. They had but to believe that God would cause the spindles to point the way they should go, and it would be so," Lee says.

Lee pauses, and John Revell picks up the narrative.

"Alma said, *'and now, my son, I would that ye should understand that these things are not without a shadow; for as our fathers were slothful to give heed to this compass—now these things were temporal—they did not prosper; even so it is with things which are spiritual.*

61

"For behold, it is as easy to give heed to the word of Christ, which will point to you a straight course to eternal bliss, as it was for our fathers to give heed to this compass, which would point unto them a straight course to the promised land.

"And now I say, is there not a type in this thing? For just as surely as this director did bring our fathers, by following its course, to the promised land, shall the words of Christ, if we follow their course, carry us beyond this vale of sorrow into a far better land of promise.... The way is prepared, and if we will look we may live forever.' Thus spoke Alma," John recites.

"And there were three witnesses of the *Liahona* in the early days and three witness in the latter-days," Dane adds.

Graham sits nodding thoughtfully. Dane looks over at his friend and lifts his hands in a shrugging motion. "Well?" he says. "See what I'm saying?"

Graham also shrugs. "Wow," he replies.

"So, here you have it. In a few words—as opposed to a whole story—it's a compass that works by faith to give moral direction as well as locational information," Dane says.

"Thank you all. I think I have a better understanding of the object and the way it works," Graham says.

"Outstanding," John says. "Any other questions?"

"Actually, I do have another question. What about your friend Matt and your covert language?" Graham asks.

"Graham..." Lee says.

"No, Lee. We need to know about him. After all, I have

the least information to fall back on, and I'm not the one holding the compass..." Graham says.

"And you're a newlywed..." Dane interjects.

"Yeah, that, too. I'd really like to know who he is before I take a very lengthy road trip with him," Graham says.

"Fair enough," John says. "Matt Tonai has been my friend for many, many years. We met a long time ago and have remained close ever since. We even studied languages together in college. That was Hebrew we were speaking—the language of the Israelites. It's fun to brush up on it when we see each other since there's nobody else we can really speak it with.

"Matt has other acquaintances who are helping us track down Dr. Fisher. In fact, one of them has been keeping tabs on the doctor all throughout Nevada, Texas, Louisiana, and Mississippi, which corresponds to what's been displaying on those spindles.

"That guy's name is Jim. He's the one who discovered the woman who is stalking the doctor. The one you called 'the she-jackal' in your track, Lee. You see, when the doctor stepped away from his practice and began traveling around, he became a gambling addict. It consumes him now, so he is going from place to place gambling and living off his winnings. That woman is following the money. We don't know who she is, and we don't know if anyone else is working with her. We only know that she is hunting him like prey."

"Whoa. That's a lot to take in," Dane says.

"It is," John says.

"So, Matt and Jim are regular private investigators? Not psychics, like us?" Graham says.

"Exactly," John says. "Matt and Jim are certainly not psychics. They are special private investigators."

"Huh. Didn't know that," Dane says.

"Now you do," Graham quips.

"I can run with that," Dane says.

"Me, too," Graham says.

"And I can accept it, as well," Lee says.

"Good. Now that it's all out in the open, can we move on tomorrow?" John asks.

"I have a question, if you will permit, John," Lee says.

"Ask away," John says.

"After I tracked, you made mention of a 'happy hunting ground.' I specifically said, 'another hunting ground.' Did you just misspeak, or did your comment have some particular significance?" Lee asks.

"Ah, I believe I misspoke, but maybe not. 'Happy hunting ground' would refer to a place of the dead. We're not sure if this woman—this she-jackal—is dangerous. I suppose I was projecting my fears when I said that," John says.

"That makes perfect sense. Thank you for clearing up my confusion," Lee says, his shoulders relaxing.

"Well, tell me this, though," Dane says, "are you independently wealthy or something? You know, you've been

64

picking up the tab for this hotel and food and gas and all."

John throws his head back and issues forth a laugh that booms like thunder and seems to come all the way up from his toes. "Yes! Yes, I am! But if you ever tell a soul, I will deny it. Mission Presidents are supposed to be paupers. I have to keep up my image," he reveals.

"You have my word, John, but I have to say that you hide it very well," Lee says.

Graham raises his hand like a schoolboy wanting to ask the teacher a question.

"Graham?" Lee says.

Graham hunches his shoulders toward his ears. "John...if you don't mind, can I order room service? I'm still hungry, and there are some really tasty sounding things on the menu that I've never tried before," he asks.

"Graham!" Lee says.

Graham shrugs. "Sorry," he mutters.

"Me, too?" Dane pipes in.

"Dane!" Lee says.

John's laugh booms again, as much from relief as from amusement. "Midnight snacks are on me. Order anything that your hearts may desire. But, bellyaches or not, we leave tomorrow at 7 a.m.," he says.

Graham and Dane leap out of their chairs and race to their room, slamming the French doors behind them. Lee and John both snicker. In a couple of seconds, they hear a timid knock at the doors. Lee cracks them open. When Dane thrusts his arm inside, Lee places the pager in his open palm.

"Good night, gentlemen," Lee says, locking the door.

From the other side, he hears the two men reading the room service menu aloud to each other, highlighting the detailed descriptions of every item on the list.

Typical, he thinks, admitting that, for once, he is glad he is not the one picking up their tab.

CHAPTER SIX

I WOULD TARRY

NOAH ENTERS THE TOMBS on the second floor of the Florida State University School of Music's main building and lets the door swing shut behind him. The corridor before him extends 40 feet before jutting off to the left for another three dozen feet, and then it takes a second left turn for 40 feet more, finally emerging into the main hall from which he entered. On either side of the U-shaped corridor are doorways. Each door opens outward from a practice room—affectionately called "practice tombs" by the FSU music students because of their tiny, cell-like feel. All are windowless save for one small one-foot by one-foot glassed in area at eye level in each heavy wooden door.

The outer practice rooms are little more than walk-in closets, six feet by eight feet in size, and furnished with one well-worn upright piano, a bench (or sometimes just a stool), a straight-backed metal chair, and a black metal music stand. These are the rooms reserved for voice majors.

The inner practice rooms are larger, eight feet by 12 feet in size. Half of them contain baby grand pianos (in much better condition) with a bench or stool at each. These are reserved for piano majors. Voice majors are never allowed the larger rooms; they are required to use the outer tombs.

A quarter of the practice rooms on the inner side are outfitted with electric organs for organ majors, and the final quarter, near the back of the U, are for instrumental groups. These rooms hold straight-back metal chairs, music stands, and battered, graffiti covered spinet pianos. The décor is the same for every practice room: a checkerboard of thick cork squares spaced out equidistantly on walls painted the color of pureed liver. They are virtually soundproof.

Beneath the windows on the outside of the heavy doors are stacks of lined sign-in papers held in place with metal clamps. Students reserve practice times often two weeks in advance, and woe be to anyone who takes a room without signing up or who, heaven forbid, crosses off someone else's name. Knock-down fist fights have been known to occur over the right to commandeer one precious hour in a practice tomb.

Noah stands looking at the series of identical doors ahead of him. Maria is here somewhere. His question is, *what kind of day is it, a voice day or a piano day?*

Maria Ramirez is a musical prodigy who had been

attending Troy State University in Alabama. This past spring, she was awarded a scholarship to the FSU School of Music and transferred to the Tallahassee-based college to be near Noah Lightfoot, whom she had met when he and the Trackers Team rescued her niece from a brutal kidnapper just over a year ago. The child was recovered unharmed, the kidnapper was killed, and 16-year-old Maria fell hard for the 18-year-old Tracker. It was love at first sight for her, and love at second sight for him.

At the time, Noah was involved with Raven Looking Bird. With Dane's restoration from death after Noah and Lee performed a psychic backtrack into the past, Raven and Dane were reunited. They married and moved to Arizona for several months where Raven gave birth to the adorable twin boys. During that time, Maria pushed any and all romantic feelings for Raven right out of Noah's head and heart. Now, the two young people are inseparable.

Walking slowly down the hall, Noah checks the sign-in sheets on either side, searching for Maria's name. He finally finds it midway down the hall after he makes the second left-hand turn. It is a voice day, and so she is in an outer room, seated at the piano, singing, with her back toward him. He cracks open the door and whistles softly so as not to scare her. She swivels on the stool and graces him with a brilliant smile that causes her soft brown eyes to squint. He swoops in and gathers her into his arms for a kiss.

"Mia, mia, mia," he murmurs into her hair, and she

giggles in return.

"What are you doing here?" she asks.

"Looking for my little songbird. Knew you were signed in. Just didn't know what kind of day it was," he says.

She grimaces. "It's a voice day. I have the WWS this afternoon," she says.

"Oh no," he commiserates, "not the Wicked Witch of the South?" He shudders dramatically.

Voice students are chosen by their vocal coaches based on their School of Music auditions. The better vocalists always get the tenured, most sought-after coaches. Maria was chosen instantly by Dr. Eva Giannella, an iconic fixture at the school, the most senior of the voice teachers, and the most demanding. A fiery Italian with an insufferable ego, she makes Maria's voice lessons miserable.

"She's trying to force me into becoming an opera diva, but I don't have the voice for it," Maria moans.

"You have the voice of an angel. She's just a hateful old bitty who's jealous of the younger talent," Noah says.

Maria sighs and hugs him tighter. "She says I sing like a toad. I have to sing *Un Bel Di* today. The aria from Puccini's opera, *Madame Butterfly*," she says.

"I've heard you sing that song. You do it beautifully, Mia. Why so worried?" he says.

"I don't do it like *she* wants it. She wants a big heavy vibrato, and I have a light airy one. Last quarter she gave me a

70

B! I've never gotten such a low grade before. Argh. Where's Graham Skysong when you need him. I bet he could sing it exactly like she wants it!" she quips.

This sends Noah into peals of laughter. "I can just picture big ole Graham, dressed in a skirt and wig, singing *One Fine Day* in a woman's voice," he says, wiping his eyes.

"You laugh, but he could do it," she retorts.

"That's the thing. I know he could. Wonder how things are going for them? I haven't heard," he says.

"I don't know, but speaking of Graham, I caught a song in my dreams last night, and I can't get it off my mind. Part of the reason I'm so stressed about my voice lesson. I can't practice my opera piece because I've got this song rolling around in my head," she says.

"Sing it for me. Maybe that'll get it out of your mind. Or maybe it's something that we might need to let the Team know about," he suggests.

She nods in agreement. "OK. I wrote it down when I woke up so I wouldn't forget the words," she says. She pulls a sheet of notebook paper from her music satchel and props it on the piano, and then she takes her seat on the stool and begins to play and sing.

Twelve Disciples tarried e're the Savior did depart.
He asked each of us to tell Him what was in our heart.
Nine men asked to come into His kingdom
when they pass. We three stood apart.

'What will you that I should do unto you three?'

We dared answer not, but He said, 'Your hearts I see.

That which you desire is what John asked of me.

You shall blessed be.

Never shall you taste of death or pain.

While I'm in my Kingdom, you three will remain.

Go and preach the Gospel,

Turn the souls of men back to God again.'

I would tarry 'til You come to earth, O Lord.

I would tarry 'til You come again.

I would travel o'er the land to preach Your word

Of salvation for all men.

Maria stops singing and looks up at Noah, surprised to see his misty eyes.

"Mia, that was...that was...wow. I don't know what that was, but it was...wow," he stammers.

She blushes and tilts her head to the side, embarrassed.

"That was like an entire song. Reminds me of 'Fiddler on the Roof' or that song Graham sings at Jewish weddings. *Hava Nagila*, I think it's called. You got that whole thing in your dream, music and words and everything?" he says.

"I got the tune and that chorus first. '*I would tarry 'til You come.*' I got that over and over. Later the other words came, and I think there might be more words to the song, but I didn't get any other verses last night. And I can't get that chorus out of my head," she says.

"Could you tell who was singing it?" Noah asks.

"Men. It was men singing. The verse was unison. The chorus was a trio, and they sang in harmony," she says.

"What about a feeling? What did your clairempathy powers make you feel?" he prompts, knowing that her dreams always bring with them feelings and emotions.

"I felt...driven, sort of. Like something was meant to happen. Anxious. Anticipating. I also felt a kind of awe and reverence, like being in church. And when they sang the chorus together, it was a feeling of brotherhood, of solidarity. Singleness of purpose. Men on a mission," she says.

"That's such a weird turn of phrase. '*I would tarry.*' Like back in Bible days," Noah says.

"Yeah, I know. Isn't it? What do you think it means? Do you think it's got something to do with Lee and that compass he found?" she says.

"Maybe. I don't know. Should probably tell them about it. Can I have that paper?" he says.

"Sure. Take it," she responds.

At that moment, the door pushes open and a pale, gangly young man pokes his head in.

"Maria Ramirez. Your time is up! I've got recital today, and I need the room," he says.

"OK, Randy. Just going," Maria says, gathering her satchel and backpack.

Randy looks over and spots Noah beside the piano.

73

"Hey, Chief! What you doin' here? You're not a voice major," he says.

Noah has an unofficial affiliation with the School of Music since he represents Chief Osceola, the Seminole Indian Chief who rides Renegade, the football team's mascot horse. Though he has a close affinity with the FSU Marching Band, he most definitely does not have a principle instrument.

"Just hanging out," Noah says with a practiced shrug.

Looking back at Maria, Randy smirks. "I get it. You're a Maria major, right?" he says.

"Yeah, yeah. Right Randy. Later, dude. C'mon Mia. I'll walk you down the yellow brick road," Noah said.

"Oh no. My condolences. You're off to see the Wicked Witch. I'll pray for you...and play for you," Randy says, pushing inside and depositing his bag on the floor. He perches on the piano stool and begins playing the opening notes to the third movement of Chopin's Sonata No. 2 in B-flat Minor, Opus 35. Maria and Noah exit the tomb to the tune of Frederic Chopin's famous Funeral March.

*   *   *

"I would tarry 'til You come to earth, O Lord," Jim sang while waiting for Doctor to come out of the convenience store. The song he and his friends composed many years ago had been on his mind all afternoon. Seeing his traveling companion exit with a sack of snacks, he yawned and settled back into his seat, ready for the next leg of the journey.

* * *

"I would tarry 'til You come again," Matt sang softly from the back seat. The travelers had stopped at a rest area for a bathroom break, and Matt returned to the van first. He popped the tab on a Sprite and took a long gulp, appreciating the convenience of cold and fizzy sweet drinks in cans.

* * *

"I would tarry," the man said as he gazed out over the grandeur of the Smoky Mountains from the mile-high Newfound Gap scenic overlook between Tennessee and North Carolina. Then, after taking another breath of the crisp, clean air, he turned and began his descent towards Gatlinburg.

* * *

"I would tarry," Kenny says. "I know those words, Noah. Luna said them to me before Dad and the others left. They're from a song? That's just bizarramundo!"

"Yep. Mia caught it last night. Thought maybe you and I might give the guys a call and see if it means anything to them," Noah says.

"They're probably on the road right now. Dad called last night and said there were some crazy developments. Get this: They're trying to track down this guy, and President Revell *knows* him! And the *Liahona* is spinning when Dad holds it, and *writing* appears on the spinners inside. And the words are in a different language, but President Revell can *read* them! Isn't that wild?" Kenny says, bouncing from side to side.

"Well, get this, little dude: Maria says there are *three men* that keep on singing this '*I would tarry*' song," Noah says.

"Noah, those may be the '*unseen*' that Luna talks about," Kenny says, standing stock-still, his smile gone.

"Whatcha mean, the '*unseen*,' Ken?" Noah asks.

"Luna told me to tell Dad, '*be mindful of the unseen*,' just before he left. She's said it a couple of times, so it must be important. Hey! I've got an idea. Why don't you track these three guys? I'll beacon for you. I'm really good at it now," Kenny suggests excitedly.

"No can do, Ken. Your mom and sisters are gone. Bill and his new family are in town. There's just you and me. No tracking with only two people. You know the rule," Noah says.

Ever since Noah was abducted, and Lee was left stranded without a beacon, it's been a hard and fast rule that nobody ever tracks without another Tracker present in case the Beacon is incapacitated. To be left without a beacon means the traveling Tracker's noncorporeal self is marooned without a means to return to the tangible confines of the body. The mortality margin is 55 minutes before a Tracker left without a mental beacon to signal the mind back will die.

"Maria?" Kenny says.

"...is trapped with that horrible troll of a voice teacher of hers at school. Not even I can pull her away from that monster," Noah says.

"Raven?" Kenny suggests.

"Nah-ah. I happen to know she and her mom took the twins to town to shop for matching baby outfits," Noah says.

"Eww. Poor little guys," Kenny commiserates.

"We'll just have to wait until somebody gets home. Maybe your dad will call in the meantime and give us some more details. Regardless, we have to tell them about the song and the men, and that maybe these unseen guys are invisible or something like that," Noah admits, moving around the kitchen, opening the oven and cabinets.

"What're you looking for?" Kenny asks.

"I'm kinda lunchy. Did your mom make anything for dinner yet? Or maybe some leftovers in the fridge?" Noah says.

"Lasagna! I think there's about four pieces left. Now that you mention it, I'm hungry, too. Cold or hot?" Kenny says, reaching for the refrigerator door.

"Cold works for me. Your mom's lasagna is killer either way," Noah says, taking a seat at the breakfast table.

Kenny brings the dish to the table and removes the tinfoil covering. "Sweet! Six pieces! Dig in," he says.

The two of them grab forks and eat directly from the casserole dish, continuing to talk and laugh as though they were both ten years old instead of 19 and almost 13.

When Wren and her three youngest daughters arrive home an hour later, hungry and craving leftovers, all they find is an empty glass Pyrex dish and two forks in the middle of the table, scraped and licked clean.

CHAPTER SEVEN

BEARS, FALLS, AND FISH

IT IS NEARLY NOON when John Revell's van passes through Pigeon Forge, Tennessee, and exits the Parkway. The winding one-way 4.3-mile road runs alongside the Little Pigeon River, taking them into Gatlinburg—the destination revealed by their morning session with the *Liahona*. John has called ahead and booked rooms for them at the Park Vista, a modern high-rise hotel high up on the mountainside, surrounded by the Smokies, with a beautiful, soaring 16-story atrium, a multi-tiered indoor pool with a waterslide, a fitness center, and a first-rate restaurant.

The Trackers' suite includes two bedrooms with a separate living room, a bathroom with a whirlpool tub, a minifridge, and an outdoor balcony with a spectacular view of the mountains in every direction. John and Matt will share a single room across the hall. Though slightly less swanky, it is richly decorated and features two queen beds, a separate sitting area, a whirlpool tub in the bathroom, a minifridge, and a balcony that sports a view of the city of Gatlinburg below.

"That's where we're staying tonight?" Graham says, his eyes on the grand hotel at the top of a steep hill.

"Looks like a huge stack of pancakes, only way more expensive," Dane notes.

"A whole lot more expensive than a stack of pancakes," John laughs, "but don't worry, they have an outstanding restaurant where I'm sure you can get a comparable stack of pancakes if you want."

"John, it is not necessary for you to expend yourself on costly hotels and food. We are quite satisfied with lesser lodgings, and these men will eat nearly anything you put before them," Lee says. Though his friend has disclosed his apparent wealth, Lee is a man of modest wants and needs.

"Believe me, I enjoy being able to treat those I care about. Besides, if I weren't intended to use my money, I wouldn't have been blessed with it. Please, let me have my fun, too," John says as they pull up to the entrance.

Acquiescing, Lee steps out of the van and stretches. The younger men grab the bags from the cargo area, and the quintet enters the hotel, noting with unfeigned appreciation the lavishness of their surroundings. When they get to their rooms, they realize the magnificence of the hotel is nothing in comparison to the splendor of the panoramic view of the surrounding Smoky Mountains. Standing on their balcony, the Trackers seem to be hovering in the treetops. They are transported into the glorious variegated greens of the woods and the wispy white clouds which give the mountains their smoky appearance. They stand speechless, for once, taking in the crisp coolness of the air and the pure clean smell of nature all around them.

"Bears!" Dane shouts, pointing to the ground.

A mere ten feet away from the hotel, although several stories down, at the edge of the tree line they see a family of black bears—a mother and four cubs. The chubby black fur balls clamber over one another, playing king of the mountain on a sapling that threatens to snap beneath their weight while their mother casually scans the parking lot for left-behind snacks from a careless guest. They are so fascinated by the bears that they fail to realize John and Matt have entered the room through the open door.

John's booming laugh thunders behind them. "Ah, you've met the local welcoming committee," he says.

"They are quite entertaining," Lee observes.

"The bears are a long-standing feature of this hotel. They've been here for as long as I've been visiting. They wait around for hand-outs from unwary guests," John says. Then, he plucks a tented cardboard flyer from the corner table and hands it to Lee. "Make no mistake. They are neither tame nor friendly. The Park Vista posts these warnings throughout the hotel for your safety."

The flyer shows a black bear with a red warning circle around it. "Do NOT attempt to feed the bears!" it reads. Lee hands it to Dane and Graham.

"Don't leave any snacks on or around the car, and don't eat while going and coming from the parking lot. The bears *will* come after you. It's their natural predisposition to search for food. Respect them, and they'll respect us," Matt advises.

"You've been here before, too?" Lee asks.

"Oh yes, many times. It's one of my favorite places on earth, right here in the mountains. I feel closer to heaven in the Smokies than just about anywhere else," Matt sighs, smiling.

"I agree," John says. "Well, how about we let our belongings lie where we deposited them in our rooms and go downstairs for some lunch? You two young fellas look to be wasting away from hunger."

"Don't have to tell me twice," Dane says, heading for the door with Graham fast on his heels.

"Shall we follow our bears?" Lee jokes.

"I should say so. Maybe we need to take this flyer with us to put beside them on the table," Matt suggests.

"Yeah. I've seen these guys eat. Be careful reaching for a plate; you'll draw back a nub!" John jokes.

* * *

As John, Matt, and the three Trackers sat down to a

hearty lunch, Dr. Fisher munched on a sandwich and Coca-Cola inside his motorhome. He had made good time, despite several stops in Alabama: Mobile, Atmore, Evergreen, and Montgomery. He slept in his motorhome at the rest area on the Georgia/Alabama border, and then he got up and fixed a breakfast of cereal, milk, and fruit. Jim had eaten his own breakfast in the wee hours of the morning before Doctor awoke. He sat waiting in the passenger seat until Doctor settled himself in the driver's seat and continued their journey through Columbus and Atlanta. Ninety minutes north of Atlanta, they arrived in the town of Tallulah Falls.

Doctor had visited Tallulah Gorge State Park many times with his wife Cheryl and the kids, Katelyn and Frankie, when they were young. It was a favorite stopover on their way to Gatlinburg and Cherokee, their other vacation destinations. The area held fond memories for him of a time when he had a happy family, before the kids had grown up and moved away to Panama City Beach.

Cheryl had succumbed to empty nest syndrome shortly thereafter. She filed for divorce three years ago and followed the children to the beach. Though she claimed she still loved him, she preferred to spend her time in the company of the kids instead of meandering around a lonely house while her husband, the renowned surgeon, spent more and longer hours at the hospital or presenting papers at conferences.

In hindsight, Dr. Jackson Fisher's celebrated career

was both a curse and a blessing. He was as much a success in one regard as he was an abject failure in the other.

He left the motorhome and entered the museum, viewing the displays he had so many times before enjoyed sharing with his family. They had not undergone many changes in these past years, and that comforted him a bit.

Located on US 441 about an hour and a half from Cherokee in North Carolina, Tallulah Falls comprised a series of waterfalls that cascaded through the Tallulah Gorge, a two-mile long 1,000-foot chasm formed by the Tallulah River cutting through the Tallulah Dome rock formation. It was commonly dubbed the "Niagara of the South" and was considered one of the Seven Natural Wonders of Georgia.

Prehistoric Indians discovered the canyon and hunted the river and deep gorge. When European settlers arrived in the 1800s, they found Cherokee Indians living there, and a legend circulated that a Cherokee warrior supposedly haunted the gorge and would frown and shoot arrows at trespassers.

Though popular belief was that the Cherokee named the churning falls *tarrurah* after the roiling river, that was a misconception. No such word existed in the Cherokee language. Their word for the river was *ugunyi*— "the terrible." Sometime before the Civil War, white settlers christened the falls Tallulah, their version of the Muskogee Creek Indian word *tvfolv,* which meant "small town with one mound."

The falls themselves were named l'Eu d'Or (Lodora),

Tempesta, Oceana, Honcon (Hurricane), the Serpentine, Bridal Veil, and Lover's Leap, the latter of which was the highest of the cliffs at 900 plus feet. Other natural formations included such delightful names as Devil's Pulpit—a 600-foot cliff overhanging the ravine, Devil's Dwelling—a 20-foot deep cave beneath Honcon, Eagle's Nest—a huge rock above a 700-foot outcropping on which eagles indeed rested, Hawthorn's Pool—named for a young English clergyman who drowned in the bottomless pool, and Hanck's Sliding Place—where a man named Hanck slipped on the rocks and slid hundreds of feet down to the floor of the ravine but miraculously survived.

Other notable facts about Tallulah Gorge and Falls had been especially interesting to Katelyn and Frankie: in 1970, 65-year-old Karl Wallenda crossed the ravine on a high wire tightrope, and—even more impressive to them—the location was featured in the Hollywood films *Deliverance* in 1972 and *Grizzly* in 1976. Though they had never seen either film because they were not allowed to attend R-rated movies, Katelyn and Frankie had heard the *"Dueling Banjos"* music from *Deliverance* on the radio. They took great pleasure in recreating the song vocally while playing air banjos whenever the family visited the park. Closing his eyes, Doctor could still hear them: *ninner nyir-nyir nyir-nyir nyir-nyir nyerrrr.*

Doctor spent a good half hour in the museum and another half hour just gazing at Oceana Falls from the scenic overlook. His view was not obstructed, but a decided mistiness prevailed as he scanned the horizon. He attributed this to fatigue and the fact that he was frequently teary-eyed from the memories; however, his vision problem was, in reality, due to his traveling companion. Beautiful as the vista was, many a depressed person had stepped over the barrier and plunged to a crushing death at the bottom. Doctor could not be allowed to follow suit, so Jim had positioned himself on the overlook in front of him. Doctor did not see Jim; he saw through him.

After a few more minutes, Doctor sighed and returned to the motorhome with Jim in tow. He pulled onto US 441 and headed for Cherokee, and Jim settled in for a short nap.

* * *

After a lunch of sumptuous proportions, the Florida travelers take in some of the local Tennessee sights. Parking at the base of the hill, they disembark the van and stroll around the quaint town of Gatlinburg on foot. Unlike the hot and humid state from which they originate, the little town of Gatlinburg offers them a cool brisk respite in a tree-filled natural setting.

Their walk takes them down the Parkway and along ladder-like rungs of short side streets that branch off the main highway. They visit abundant tourist shops that sell trinkets and keepsakes labeled "*Smoky Mountains*" and a seemingly unlimited supply of t-shirts with images and quips that run the gamut from innocuous to suggestive.

John and Matt, as long-time visitors, know the best

places to browse, and they take the Trackers to their favorite spots. The men take the opportunity to buy small meaningful gifts for their families. While they make their purchases throughout the relaxing day, they take advantage of the various food vendors on the strip, despite having eaten a huge lunch, and not worried a bit about spoiling their appetites for dinner.

Knowing Wren's fondness for sweets, Lee purchases two pounds of fudge for her at the *Ole Smoky Candy Kitchen* and a large sack of freshly pulled taffy for the kids. He holds tightly to the sack, lest the human bears that accompany him get hold of the candies and eat them all.

Graham carefully considers everything he sees in each shop they visit, but it is not until they step into the *Beneath the Smoke* art gallery that he finds exactly the right gift for Shine. He leaves the shop with a framed photograph—signed by the photographer—of a family of black bears in the woods with the misty clouds from the mountains all around them. Graham is comforted in the fact that the photograph cannot ever be sung into existence by a corrupted Blessing Way song the way the sand paintings were in their recent New Mexico adventure.

Their final shopping destination turns out to be their favorite, and the men enjoy roaming around the small stores inside the *Mountain Mall* on the Parkway, a three-story building that houses museums, art galleries, camping outfitters, curio shops, and food vendors. In one tiny closet-sized booth, Dane finds a beautifully carved *kachina* for Raven, a piece of painted pottery for his mother-in-law Robin, and hand-made leather-tooled teething rattles for the babies.

The men's day in the Smoky Mountain town passes quickly, and as the sun begins to set, they duck into a local hole-in-the-wall restaurant for supper. Named *Catch of the Day*, the specialty of the house is always fish caught that day in one of the nearby mountain waterways.

Seating themselves at a round table for six, the Trackers appraise their surroundings, noting with approval the red gingham curtains and the red plaid cloths on the heavy wooden tables set with locally made pottery dishes in pale, blue hues. In the center of the table are four round hand thrown crocks with lids, each sporting a tiny ceramic spoon. Graham is about to lift the lid on the dark yellow crock when a cheery white-haired waitress approaches the table. She holds no menus, nor does she have an order pad—just a large cobalt blue ceramic pitcher of ice water.

"Welcome to *Catch of the Day*, gentlemen," she drawls brightly, expertly filling their glasses with both water and ice.

"Hello, Sally," John says with a smile.

"Why, hello yourself, dear. So glad to have you back with us," she says, and then she sees Matt. "And welcome back to you too, honey. Haven't seen you here for a while."

"Glad to be here, Ms. Sally," Matt says.

"There are five of us, but these two eat like three," John says, indicating Graham and Dane.

"Oh, you got here just at the right time. We got two granddaddies today. I'll go earmark them for you," she says, scurrying off to the kitchen.

"Um, isn't she going to get our order?" Dane asks.

"She already did," Matt responds. "Dinner for six."

Graham and Dane exchange puzzled looks, then they both lift their heads and let their extrasensory powers go to work—Dane sniffing deeply, and Graham craning his head around to hear the kitchen conversation.

"Happy people. Satisfied diners. Kitchen staff polite and joking with one another. '*I need them two granddaddies for my table*,' Sally says. '*You got it, Sal*,' someone responds," Graham relates to his tablemates.

"And I smell fish...but I only detect one type of fish," Dane says puzzled.

"Rainbow trout," John says. "*Catch of the Day* serves only rainbow trout."

"That's unusual," Lee remarks.

"Not when you taste it, you won't think it's unusual. They do one thing, and they do it right," Matt says.

"I also smell roast potatoes, a fried corn bread, and a kind of cruciferous green vegetable. Broccoli?" Dane says.

"Have to wait and see," John says.

"I take it they serve precisely the right amount of trout for the guests at the table," Lee says.

"Yep. And the rest of the food comes family-style in

large serving bowls and platters," Matt says.

"So, no taking orders, no remembering anything except the number of people eating. I get it. Seems pretty simple," Graham says.

"And dessert is always apple cobbler," John says.

"OK by me," Dane says with a grin.

In less than half an hour, two servers appear carrying twin platters which they set on the table for the men to view. The hand-made iridescent platters are about 24 inches by 12 inches, and each one holds an entire grilled rainbow trout with gleaming skin mimicking the glaze of the serving dish.

As the men stare in awe at the beautifully presented fish, the servers perform their magic in tandem. Placing long, thin two-pronged forks just behind each fish's heads, they twist the implements back toward the tail, rolling and pulling the gleaming skin off without damaging the flesh beneath. Forks and skin are then deposited onto an empty platter. As soon as the skin is removed, Dane's mouth waters at the strong aroma of the perfectly cooked trout.

The next step involves sliding a sharp knife beneath the flesh at the tail and carefully deboning the fillet. When the knife reaches the head, one server uses a flat spatula-type instrument to deposit the top portion of the fish onto Graham's plate. The second server divides the other fillet into three equal portions and serves them to Matt, John, and Lee. The head and skeleton are removed to the extra platter.

The servers then slide the sharp knives beneath the bottom fillets, severing the skin. Dane is served the single fillet, and the other men are again served equal portions of the remaining fish. The whole process takes less than six minutes and is done with surgical precision, after which the servers remove the platters of skin and bones.

Sally is immediately behind them and begins placing three large serving bowls onto the table. One holds red, white, and purple fingerling potatoes which are roasted and salted. Another holds cornbread fritters cooked in cast iron molds shaped like seashells. The last holds bright green steamed Romanesco broccoli—the edible flower buds of a particular species of broccoli—standing up like tiny Christmas trees.

"Here at *Catch of the Day*, we celebrate the rainbow trout in nature. The blue plates represent the cool mountain streams and rivers they swim in. These potatoes represent the colored river rocks where they lay their eggs. The broccoli, grown right here at our farm, represents the trees in the woods. And these corn fritters represent shells of crustaceans found in the water," Sally says beaming. "I hope you enjoy everything."

Impressed, the gentlemen show their appreciation by clapping, a common sound heard throughout the restaurant as the customers are served.

"They make eating an adventure," Lee says.

"What about these crocks on the table? What do they stand for?" Dane asks.

"Oh, I can tell you," Matt says. "The bright yellow one is clarified drawn butter, representing the fish living a happy fat life. The pale yellow one is lemon juice, representing the sour feeling of being caught."

"The white one is salt for the savoring of life, and the black one is pepper, for the bitterness of loss," John says.

"Oh, wow. That's kinda sad," Dane says. He notices the amused looks on the faces of the others. "Wait, is that for real or are you guys jerking my chain?"

Graham puts his index finger into the side of his mouth and pulls, mimicking a fish caught on a hook. "You've been had, Dane. They're putting you on," he says.

"What *are* they, then?" Dane asks.

"They're condiments, man. They're just seasonings," Graham says. "Eat your fish and shut up."

John claps Dane on the back good-naturedly, and they all get down to the business of devouring every morsel of their food. When their plates are empty, the servers return and bus the table. Sally presents a tray laden with a large red-glazed casserole dish of hot apple cobbler. She scoops healthy portions into five matching smaller bowls and leaves the rest in the dish for those who want seconds.

A server brings each of them an eight-ounce milk bottle full of ice-cold cream and refills their water glasses. No strangers to cobbler, the Trackers immediately pour the cream over their desserts. John and Matt follow suit.

"I see y'all know to eat cobbler the right way," Sally says with a wink.

"My wife makes a delicious cobbler that tastes very much like this one, ma'am," Lee says.

"I bet it's the same Southern recipe. *Sticka-cuppa-cuppa-cuppa-canna-350?*" Sally asks.

"Exactly!" Lee exclaims.

"My granny taught me that way. Melt a *sticka* butter in the dish. Mix a *cuppa* flour, a *cuppa* sugar, and a *cuppa* milk together and then pour it in the butter. Drop a *canna* apple pie filling all around the dish, but don't you dare stir it! The batter will come up and cover the apples as it bakes in a 350° oven," Sally says. "That your wife's recipe?"

Lee nods his head vigorously, his mouth full of cobbler.

"The butter sort of fries it at the same time, you know, giving the crust that crispiness. The only difference is that here we use fresh apples from the farm cooked down with cane sugar instead of the canned filling, and I like to grate in some fresh cinnamon off the stick. But the same ole cobbler either way. Glad you enjoy it," she says.

After eating their fill of the main course and dessert, the five men wander back to the van and return to the Park Vista, anxious to talk to their loved ones and get some rest before tomorrow's journey, which will inevitably take them farther northward—farther from their families, yet closer to Dr. Fisher and the quest set forth by the *Liahona*. Where they are headed, only the ancient compass knows, but one thing is for certain: nobody orders room service tonight...except the sixth man, who slips into the room behind John and Matt, unseen by the three Trackers.

CHAPTER EIGHT
<u>OCONALUFTEE</u>

EARLY THE NEXT MORNING, Dr. Jackson Fisher stepped outside his motorhome and stretched, looking around at the other recreational vehicles set up in the River Valley Campground where he spent the night. The air was chilly enough for a long-sleeved shirt, but Doctor savored the coolness as he sipped his coffee.

The campground had been owned and operated by the same Cherokee family since 1964, and Doctor had stayed there with his family many times. It featured hiking trails, a waterfall, nearby tubing and river swimming, and excellent fishing, all of which his family had sampled and enjoyed. But the painful realization that they would never again stay here as a family made the hot coffee turn bitterly unpleasant in his mouth. He abruptly spat it on the ground and reentered the RV.

Might as well make a day of bitter memories, he thought as he pulled out of his parking spot and headed onto the main road. His first stop was Mountain Farm Museum, a collection of old farm buildings which were relocated from throughout the Smoky Mountains onto a low-lying valley as an historical preservation to replicate an old farmstead.

Doctor strolled leisurely through the barn, the springhouse, an apple house, and a smoke house that had been arranged as they would have been over a century ago. The buildings were set up as if their owners had just stepped away, leaving a realistic tableau of their lifestyle. There was fresh water in a covered barrel in the springhouse, along with a stack of paper cups for those who wanted a drink. Ripe red apples were piled in a wooden bin in the apple house—free for visitors to grab as a sweet, juicy snack. Fragrant meat hung from hooks in the smoke house, which sported a wooden box of beef jerky smoked the night before—also free for the taking.

Doctor was always humbled at the way people had eked out a living for themselves without the convenience of modern tools and electricity. He examined the workmanship of the barn, which was pegged together instead of nailed. Seeing graffiti etched deeply into the walls and beams of the 100-year-old buildings, he was saddened. Those early pioneers would never have desecrated their homes that way. Shaking his head, he moved off toward the grain mill where there was a corn grinding demonstration in progress.

Jim, too, was sad, but his melancholia went much deeper. He remembered living in a house very much like the cabin they visited. At the time, he had a wife and children, and they farmed a similar homestead. Jim had constructed all the buildings himself.

He ran his hands over the rough-hewn wood post on the porch and closed his eyes. In his memories, he heard the cow lowing, smelled the hay in the mule's stall, tasted the sticky sweet syrup of the crushed sugar cane. He recalled cutting four-inch sticks of cane for his children to chew—a favorite treat. And he remembered the joy on Amelia's face, running breathless over the hill with an armful of wildflowers to put in the pitcher on the table. But that was a lifetime ago. He turned and followed Doctor back to the RV, knowing the next stop would hold more bittersweet memories.

A short drive away was the entrance to the *Oconaluftee* Indian Village. A "living" museum, as opposed to the static displays in the farm, the village showed what a Cherokee Indian community would have been like in 1760.

During the eighteenth and nineteenth centuries, the Cherokee had a tenuous relationship with European settlers. Skirmishes resulted from the strain of two different ethnic groups of people trying to coexist: one group claimed their ownership of the land had been in place for many hundreds of years; the other group, seeing no written deeds, staked out their claims as newcomers. Often, there was bloodshed, and more than a few settlers' wives and children ended up "adopted" by the Cherokee when the men were killed.

Despite the fierce challenges, the American Indian community survived, and the town of Cherokee became the home of the Eastern Band of the Cherokee Nation, located on some 57,000 acres they purchased with the help of a white man, and which was held in trust for them by the federal government. This large tract of land was mostly dense woods and mountains in western North Carolina, near the present-day Great Smoky Mountains National Park, and it was named the *Qualla* Boundary.

A dramatic retelling of the Cherokee's existence from the 1800s to the present was conceived in 1950, and the story was presented nightly each summer at the Mountainside Theater, an outdoor amphitheater that seated thousands of people. *"Unto These Hills"* featured a cast of hundreds of Cherokee and Caucasian performers who sang, acted out battle scenes, and staged a compelling narrative of the early residents of the area.

Doctor and his family had attended the performance one summer; Jim had lived it for many summers.

The two men first browsed the Museum of the Cherokee Indian, which presented Cherokee culture, art, and history as exhibits, holographs, photographs, and films, and also sold numerous books about the tribe and the area. Leaving the museum, they entered the *Oconaluftee* demonstration village. Throughout the village, a score of traditionally attired participants interacted with guests and made pottery, shot darts out of long blowguns, ground corn with a heavy post in a hollowed-out stump, and wove baskets with straw, reeds, stripped tree bark, or pine needles—all of which were for sale.

Doctor stopped to watch a canoe being hulled out of a nine-foot section of a whole tree. The process was fascinating: The log was chipped out in the center to make a deep depression, and then live coals were placed in the depression and fanned. As the coals burned, the ashes were scraped away, more coals were added, and the process was repeated over and over. At the same time, another man shaped the ends of the log to make them narrower and rounded so the canoe could move more quickly on the water. Jim flexed his hands. He had been burned often while making such a canoe.

Leaving the demonstration, Doctor made his way to a rounded rivercane and mud plaster building with a thatched roof of poplar bark. Benches had been set up along the walls inside the *adanelá tsunilawisdi*—or meeting longhouse—for guests to sit while a white-haired man explained how their homes were made. He relayed other historical information, such as the difference between the white Cherokee bands (peaceful) and the red Cherokee bands (warlike).

Jim was thankful for the bench and the coolness inside the meetinghouse. He sat alone, across from Doctor and some other guests, and stretched his long legs out in front of him.

His own wattle and daub thatched roof *asi* house had been exactly like this, only smaller.

Jim had lived with the Cherokee for quite a few years, but he stayed away from the groups who insisted on making war with the white men. He was a peaceful man. Though he never participated in the fighting, the others did not seem to notice. Whenever a war party was formed, Jim simply willed himself to be unseen, and when they returned, they never realized he had not been with them.

After one such battle, his kinsmen came home with some "adoptees." The women and children they brought were always well treated, but many never adapted to the Cherokee lifestyle, and they often unsuccessfully tried to run away. When they were caught and returned, some stopped eating or found other permanent means of escape from their captive lives.

On that day, Jim stepped outside his home and came face to face with a girl of about 16. She was dirty and crying, her clothing was torn, and her hair had come loose from its ribbon ties. Jim was struck by her beauty. Her hair flying around her small face was the color and texture of fine corn silk, and when he looked into her tear-filled eyes the color of the summer sky, he fell instantly in love with her.

He was not married when he began his mission, and it had never held a place of importance in his life. But on that day, he knelt inside his small house and prayed.

"Almighty One, I have been faithful for these many

years, and I have traveled far and wide alone among your children. I ask that you grant me a season of time to live as other men, to take unto me a wife, and to raise up posterity. If you would grant me this request, I humbly thank you; however, in all things, I accept your will," he said.

Immediately, he felt a warmth come over him, and it seemed he heard a voice saying, "*You have been faithful, Shemnon. I grant you a season to do as you desire. At the end of that season, it is my will that you continue your mission. Go and take your wife.*"

Shemnon arose and found the elders of the village. They agreed to give him the new captive as his woman. Over the years, Amelia gave him seven sons. They lived for a time at the *Qualla,* and the oldest sons remained and took wives of their own. The three youngest boys went with Shemnon and Amelia when they left the Cherokee and traveled to a valley farther east to farm the land. When Amelia died, Shemnon brought his youngest son—the blue-eyed one like his mother—back to the *Qualla* to live because he had heard the voice say, *"Shemnon, your season has ended. Do my will."* That was centuries ago.

As Jim reminisced, he did not notice the small girl who came over and sat beside him. She was about five years old, dressed in traditional clothing, and her hair was pulled back into a tight braid. She stuck her skinny legs out in front of her, imitating Jim's pose. Jim pulled his legs back and sat up. She did the same. He turned and looked at her, and she grinned.

Jim glanced around the room. He was hidden from all the other guests, yet this little girl saw him. He was puzzled. *How do you see me, little one?* he wondered. She giggled at his consternation. Then, she climbed down off the bench and looked up at him. Taking his hand, she planted a kiss on his palm, and then skipped away out the door.

Doctor was also leaving the meetinghouse, so Jim followed him as he joined a crowd of people who were gathered in front of a sash finger-weaving demonstration. While Doctor watched, Jim scanned the grounds for the child who had interacted with him when he should have been unseen.

Looking back up, Jim was alarmed to see a woman pressed up close to Doctor. She was wearing blue jean shorts and a tight pink t-shirt. A baseball cap covered her head, and her light brown ponytail stuck out the opening in the back. The two of them appeared to be engaged in conversation, so Jim moved closer. Then he heard the woman laugh, and he saw her touch Doctor's arm.

Covetress! A bag of nickels would do me no good here, he realized. The woman casually patted Doctor's back with her left hand as she pointed a finger of her right hand toward the demonstration, misdirecting his attention. She slowly moved her other hand toward the side pocket of his lightweight windbreaker—the pocket that held his RV keys. Several people stood between Doctor and himself, and Jim tried earnestly to skirt them without being detected.

Suddenly, the little girl from the meetinghouse came forward and took the evil woman's free hand, pulling her toward the demonstration.

"Ah, our small one has found a volunteer. Here you go, lady. Hold your hands out in front of you with your fingers outstretched. Yes, that's it. And now let's loop the yarn around them, like so, and we will hand weave a special sash just for you and your gentleman friend," the old woman said.

Covetress tried to pull away, but the little girl quickly stepped beneath her arms and reached up, grasping her wrists, holding them still and keeping the woman from moving.

"Stop, you little beast. I don't want to make a sash," she hissed, trying to pull out of the child's grip, but the girl held on with surprising strength.

"She says I'm the best, and she wants to make a sash," the child announced.

The audience laughed and clapped, watching the old woman weave the yarn in and around the unwilling fingers of the struggling woman. It was not a quick process, and Doctor soon grew bored and walked away, leaving *Covetress* caught in the clutches of the child.

Jim hurriedly caught up to Dr. Fisher and stayed by his side all the way back to the RV. On his way toward the parking lot, he noticed that several villagers of all ages looked at him when he passed, as though they—like the little girl—could see him. He was sure he was still hidden, but a husky young man turned from his blowgun demonstration and nodded at him, a bent old woman with pale blue eyes threw her crab-like hand in the air and waved, and two children stopped playing fetch with a rambunctious puppy to gaze in his direction.

At first Jim was confused, and then he understood: *these are my posterity.* And for the first time in a very long time, he was happy.

CHAPTER NINE
<u>HOME TRACK</u>

LOVIE, THE AFRICAN CIVET, flexes her paws open and closed after her sharp claws are clipped and filed by Shine, and then she curls herself up in her owner's lap.

"That thing still freaks me out, you know," Raven says. When Raven began tracking after her reunion with Dane, one of the first pictures she drew while in her trance was of a civet in a cage, along with a tiny silver spoon. The animal was Lovie's mother, and she had died of trauma after her anal glands were scraped with the spoon to harvest a substance used as a fixative in high-end perfumes. Graham rescued the pup and gave it to Shine as an engagement present. A talented veterinarian technician, Shine is perfectly equipped to tame the wild creature and domesticate her as a pet.

"But she's really sweet, Raven," Shine says.

"Oh, it's not that. I just keep seeing the picture I drew. And you have to admit, with those stripes and spots and long nose, she looks like a cat morphed with a racoon," Raven says.

"Not to mention that she laughs like a human. If that doesn't wig you out, nothing should," Kenny says.

"I've gotta say, Shine, I've never seen Graham's place look so good. Even the dishes are washed, and the bed is made," Noah says, dropping down on the sofa beside Maria.

"And what're you doing in their bedroom Mr. Nosy?" Maria says, punching him in the arm.

"I had to see a man about a dog," he replies.

"What?" Maria says.

"Don't even ask," Raven warns, rolling her eyes.

The four Trackers left in Florida are gathered at Graham's and Shinehah's modest home. Because the Thistleseed house is jam packed with people, Kenny suggested they use the Skysong home as a quiet and neutral place for them to compare notes and do some tracking of their own. Shine is delighted. She misses her new husband, so being in the company of her friends and her little brother makes her less lonely. She has even baked four dozen chocolate chip cookies, knowing that Kenny and Noah are bottomless pits.

"So, here's the deal," Kenny says. "I talked to Dad last night, and there are some strange things happening. Not that my father using the ancient *Liahona* to guide him on a quest isn't strange enough, right?"

105

"Ya think?" Noah quips.

"Yeah. Well, anyway. Dad said Mr. Revell met up with an old friend at the hotel their first night, and now that guy is traveling with them," Kenny informs them.

"I know. Dane told me about him. That's pretty bizarre," Raven says.

"You ain't heard bizarre, yet. This guy and Mr. Revell talk to each other in another language. They said it was Hebrew, but it really isn't. It's something like it, though. Ara…Ara…Dang it! Forgot the word," Kenny says.

"Aramaic," Maria states.

"That's it! How'd you know?" Kenny exclaims.

Maria looks at Noah, and he shrugs. "I've been catching dreams of three men singing in English and in an ancient language. I told Noah some of the words I heard, and he made a trip to the Linguistics Department at FSU and found out it's Aramaic," she says.

"Wow," Raven says. "What's Aramaic?"

"It's the ancient language of the Jews. Back in the time of Jesus. It's what they spoke before they spoke Hebrew," Maria says, "and pretty much nobody speaks it anymore."

"Graham told me the same thing. He heard them speaking this language, but Mr. Revell explained it away," Shine says.

"Graham knows Aramaic?" Maria asks.

"No, but Gray has sung for Jewish weddings, so he

knew it wasn't regular Hebrew," Shine explains.

"Oh! Ah ha! I'm seeing the bizarreness now. What else is happening?" Raven says.

"I want to know about this other man," Shine says.

"Oh, yeah, Matt something. Him and John Revell went to college together and studied languages, or so they say. Dad's not too keen on that story or the chance meeting either," Kenny says.

"They've seen him? Talked to him?" Noah asks.

"Well, duh, Noah. I guess so," Raven responds.

"Wait, I know where he's coming from, Raven. Luna told me to tell Dad to '*mind the unseen.*' Noah's wondering if he's unseen. The answer is no, he's not unseen. They see him and talk with him," Kenny says.

"Anything else strange going on?" Shine asks.

"Well, did you guys know that Mr. Revell is rich?" Kenny asks.

Shine and Raven exchange glances. "We did, but the guys told us not to say anything," Raven says.

"Oh, hey. Thanks a lot. I get to be the last to know?" Noah is disgruntled and pokes his lips out in a pout.

"I'm sorry, Noah. Graham made me promise," Shine apologizes. She pushes a platter toward him on the coffee table. "Here, have another cookie."

He snatches two from the plate and stuffs them in his mouth, then he drains his glass of milk and pushes it toward her. Shine laughs and gets up to refill his glass. This is his way of showing he isn't really upset.

"I have something I need to tell you," Maria says to them. She reaches into the pocket of her shorts and pulls out a folded piece of notebook paper. "I dreamed more of the song."

Shine sets Noah's milk down on the coffee table and sits back in her chair, settling Lovie on her lap again. Raven, Kenny, and Noah stare at Maria expectantly as she opens the paper and smooths out the creases.

"Just gonna read it instead of singing. OK?" she says. Hearing no objections, she begins reciting what she's written.

> *We were cast in prison,*
> *thrown in pits deep in the ground,*
> *locked up with wild beasts,*
> *but what the foolish people found,*
> *though they tried to burn and kill us,*
> *we still walked around unharmed, healthy, free.*
> *We did what the Christ commanded us to do,*
> *preaching to the Nephites and tribes of Israel, too,*
> *teaching them the gospel, both Gentile and Jew.*
> *They shall blessed be.*
> *Never shall we taste of death or pain.*
> *While He's in his kingdom, we three will remain.*
> *Go and preach the gospel, turn the souls of men*
> *Back to God again.*

Maria scans the faces of her friends for any sign of

recognition or understanding. Kenny has gone ghostly white.

"Kenny? What is it? What does it mean?" she asks.

Kenny stands up and heads for the kitchen. "I need a drink of water," he mumbles, his voice cracking.

Maria, Raven, and Noah sit patiently waiting for his return, and then they hear the back door close. Shine peeks through the window. "Give him a few minutes. This is a lot to digest," she urges.

"Do you know what it means, Shine?" Raven asks.

"I think I do, but it seems impossible. I'm not a storyteller like Dad, but if the song you're hearing is what I think it is...oh well, here goes." She takes a deep breath and then exhales raggedly before continuing. "You know we're Latter-day Saints, and there are stories in the Book of Mormon that we've grown up with. One of them is about three Nephite disciples who are immortal."

"Time out. What's a Nephite disciple?" Noah asks.

"Nephites were ancient people who migrated to the new world—America—from the middle east. They were named after a prophet, Nephi, who was the son of Lehi—the man who found and first used the *Liahona*. There were 12 disciples who followed Jesus when he came to America. When it was time for him to leave, he asked them all what they wanted from him. Nine of them wanted to go to Heaven and be with Jesus after they died, but three of them asked to remain on earth until he came again," Shine says.

"Like St. John the Beloved?" Maria asks.

"Exactly," Shine confirms.

"Shine, you and Maria are Christians, but Noah and I are not believers. This sounds really made up," Raven says.

"I know, Raven. It's a lot to swallow, but it's part of our religion," Shine acknowledges.

"As a Catholic, I know all about the disciple John who Christ loved so much he entrusted his mother Mary into his keeping as he was being crucified. John asked to remain on earth until the Savior's return. It sounds like these three men in the Thistleseed's religion asked the same thing," Maria says.

"They shall tarry until his coming. They shall never suffer death or sorrow but will have the fulness of joy. They shall minister to the Gentiles, Jews, and scattered tribes of Israel and shall go throughout all nations preaching Christ's message. They shall have the ability to be unseen by men unless it is their desire to be visible," Kenny says from the doorway. His face is pale, and the tracks of shed tears are fresh on his cheeks.

For once, all the young people are silent. Finally, Noah speaks. "Ken? Are you all right?" he asks.

Kenny sits down cross-legged on the floor and nods. "I am as all right as I can be, I guess. Luna confirms what I thought. The three disciples have something to do with my dad's quest. There's a woman involved, and she's super evil. Dad called her "the she-jackal" in his track. Luna says she is more than human. She's really bad news. I think Mr. Revell and his friend probably know about the three guys and the woman, too. I think maybe they're keeping an eye out, you know? Keeping Dad and Dane and Graham safe," he says. Looking up, he gives a wan smile. "But I know something else about the Nephite disciples: Satan has no power over them."

Shine and the four young Trackers take in this news soberly. Then Noah, the unofficial leader in Lee's absence, takes charge. "OK. Here's what we're gonna do. We track. As always, I'll go first and get a look at Lee and the other guys. Ken, you light my way. When I return, then I want you, Raven, to track that jackal. Draw her in detail, OK? Mia, you beacon for Raven. You're ready for it. Shine, you go lock all the doors and windows, and then you keep watch. Make sure nobody is alone. Nobody. You all understand? Let's do this," Noah says.

He leans back on the couch and begins taking slow breaths. Kenny, on the floor, closes his eyes and rests his head on his chest. Soon, the two of them are breathing in unison while the girls watch. Five minutes later, Noah sucks in a deep breath. "Home," he sighs, and then he opens his eyes. Kenny lifts his head and opens his own eyes. Noah fixes his gaze on the opposite wall and begins relating the track he's witnessed with his photographic memory.

"They are in Revell's van. He's driving. Lee sits in the passenger seat. Behind them sit Graham and Dane. Both of them appear to be napping. Dane's mouth is open, so I'm

111

pretty sure he's asleep. In the seat behind them is another man. Must be Revell's friend. He is tan with curly black hair. He appears to be asleep, too, but his mouth is moving. He's talking in his sleep. The luggage is in the cargo area behind him. Ooh, and shopping bags! I think we're getting presents! Everyone seems relaxed. I don't sense any danger," he says.

"That's great. My turn," Raven says. She has spread some blank notebook paper on the coffee table and sits poised over them, pencil in hand. She and Maria both close their eyes and sync their breathing. Soon, Raven begins sketching on the paper. Her movements are jerky at first, and then she uses smoother strokes as images begin to form. Knowing her style, Noah hovers nearby and, sure enough, she wears the pencil point down flat. He plucks it from her hand and places another in her fingers deftly, not disturbing her drawing at all. Raven hesitates a moment, and Noah pulls the paper away, so she has a clean sheet on which to continue. She fills the sheet with sketches, and then she abruptly sits back. "Get me home," she calls. Immediately both Raven's and Maria's eyes open.

All five of them hunch over the table, examining the drawings and making comments. The first page is covered with images of a woman's face, but with different styles of light and dark hair. In one image, the shape of her jaw is square, and her dark eyes are slanted slightly. The full mouth is turned up in a hideous smile in some views; in others, her mouth is tight-lipped and thin, her face is rounder, and her eyes are lighter.

One view shows her in mid scream, exposing sharp canine teeth, a furious expression contorting her features.

"The she-jackal." Kenny's voice is emotionless.

"A mistress of disguises, it appears," Shine says.

Maria shudders, and then she pulls the other paper into view. This picture is not of the woman; it is of the passengers in John Revell's van. The point of view is from above, and they can see Revell driving and Lee engaged in conversation with him. Dane and Graham are in the seats behind them. Dane's mouth is, indeed, open. Graham's head is resting against the window. Looking closer, Shine notices something interesting.

"Gray is not asleep," she says.

"What? How can you tell?" Noah asks.

"When my husband sleeps, his face is relaxed, and the tip of his tongue protrudes from his mouth," she says. "Look at this picture. His jaw is clenched. No tongue sticking out at all. He's not asleep. He's listening!"

"Go Graham," Kenny laughs.

They examine the man sitting on the bench seat behind Graham. His head is laid against the seat, facing inward, his mouth slightly open.

"Yo, Raven. You smudged your picture," Noah says.

Beside the man in the back, the seat appears blurred. Raven squints at it.

"Nope. I draw what I see, Noah. I saw a blur right there," she says.

"If you say so. I'm thinking you maybe smudged it with your hand. No big deal. At least we can see everybody, and they look like they're OK," Noah says. "I'm ready for more cookies…or lunch, even. How about you guys?"

They congregate in the kitchen as Shine begins pulling out lunch meats, cheese, condiments, and a loaf of bread for sandwiches. Their minds at ease, they will relate the findings of their tracks to the men when they make their evening calls.

Kenny remains behind in the living room and continues looking at the picture with the smudge, wondering. And he hears Luna's telepathic voice insistently speaking in his head. *Mind the unseen, Chenaniah. Mind the unseen.*

CHAPTER TEN

THE UNSEEN

THE SIXTH MAN WATCHES THE DROOL seep from the corner of Mathoni's mouth and presses his own lips together to keep from laughing aloud. *Mathoni, the pretty one. Mathoni, the healer. Mathoni, the gift. What a gift!* he thinks. *After all these years, you still talk in your sleep.* The unseen man listens to his friend intently, just in case Mathoni discloses something unintentionally. It has always been somewhat of a concern. Even so, he loves him like a brother...like his own brothers, long since passed beyond the veil.

He shifts his attention to the other men in the van. The ponytailed one in the seat in front of him snores. Every few minutes he wiggles his nose like a hare, as though sniffing the air around him, but he continues to slumber soundly.

The burly one, though. He appears to sleep, but he is

feigning sleep in order to listen to the sounds within the vehicle. Because of this, the sixth man is careful to be absolutely still, despite the cramp working its way into his calf. If he moves, the burly one will hear.

Though unseen by the other passengers, the sixth man catches John Revell's eye as he glances back in the rearview mirror. John nods and begins scanning the roadside, looking for a place to stop.

"I'm going to need to pull over for a bit, Lee. I need to stretch my legs," John says.

"That is perfectly fine, John. I could use a good walk myself," Lee admits.

John finds a grassy shoulder and eases the van off the roadway, cruising to a gentle stop. Turning off the engine, he addresses his passengers.

"Are we there yet?" Dane mumbles.

"No, just making a stop," Graham says.

"Hey, fellas. Let's take a couple minutes and get some fresh air, walk around a bit, maybe consult the compass again. What do you say?" John says.

"Good for me, John," Graham says, "I'm a little cramped up back here anyway."

"Yeah, me too," Dane yawns, "and I need to step back behind those trees for a second, if you know what I mean."

"Wake up, Matt. Taking a stretch break," John calls.

Everyone disembarks from the vehicle. Matt rustles

around, clearing his throat, kicking the seat, and making noises as he hops out of the van, covering up the sound of the sixth man getting out. He leaves the side door standing open.

As soon as Dane returns from his business behind the trees, the men gather around Lee. He holds the *Liahona* in his cupped hands and studies the spindles within the ball.

"I do not believe there is any change," Lee says.

John stares into the center of the compass and nods vigorously in agreement.

"Yep. Same as before. New York. Just a few more hours. Well, at least the weather will be a bit cooler," he says.

Dane has visibly paled. "I don't care much for New York, Hona," he says. New York City was where he and Noah were mugged. His long hair was forcibly cut off before the brothers were saved by a Jamaican cab driver wielding a baseball bat. Dane has no interest in returning to that scene.

"I understand, Dane. But I believe this is upstate New York. Is that what you said, John?" Lee says.

"Yes. Much farther upstate and off to the west. We'll stop in Syracuse. Away from New York City, Dane," John confirms sympathetically.

"OK. Good," Dane says, grasping his ponytail and holding it tightly against his neck.

"Lee, in your track this morning, you mentioned a boundary of flags near the hunting grounds by a crooked body of water. Did we ever decide where that might be?" Graham asks, consulting his notepad.

"No. I do not think we did, Graham. Perhaps that is information that will reveal itself at our next track," Lee says.

"But we're not stopping again, except for stretch breaks, until we get to New York, is that right?" Graham asks.

"That is correct, Graham," Lee says.

"I've already booked rooms for us at the Marriot Downtown Syracuse. Don't worry, Dane. It's a large hotel and self-contained. We won't even have to go into the city unless you want to shop," John says.

Dane manages a wan smile, still clutching his ponytail. "No thanks. I'm good," he says.

The men walk around for a few more minutes, getting the kinks out from prolonged sitting, discussing options, and comparing notes. As they focus on their conversations, they are unaware of the movements of the sixth man.

Jonas, called Joe in this dispensation of time, quietly attends to his own bathroom break before reentering the van through the open door. Because he is hidden unless he wants to be seen, he simply relieves himself next to the vehicle. He doesn't want to chance walking near the burly man with the enhanced hearing. Besides, passing motorists cannot see him, so he is in no danger of offending anyone.

Quietly reentering the van, he eschews one of the cold and sweet fizzy drinks in a can of which Mathoni is so fond because of the noise it would make. Instead, he gulps down a chilled bottled water before placing the empty container beneath the seat. Likewise, he avoids the ham sandwiches from the cooler in the back for fear of crinkling the wax paper in which they are wrapped. Thankfully, he can quickly eat the hamburger that Mathoni has removed from its packaging and left for him on the back seat. Thus renewed, he scoots over and makes himself comfortable against the window behind Dane's seat, waiting for the other men to return.

Soon, John and Matt return to the van and rummage around noisily in the cooler, grabbing sodas and sandwiches for everyone. When they are all settled in, John pulls back onto the highway.

Dane twists his head around and regards Graham. "Hey, did you get a burger? I only got a sammich," he says.

"Nope. Ham sandwich for me," Graham states.

"Who got a burger?" Dane asks sniffing the air.

"Oh, sorry, Dane. I hadn't finished mine from earlier today. Left it out of the cooler, so I threw it out. Didn't think it was any good," Matt says.

"Hmph. You could've asked, dude. I'd have eaten it," Dane says grumpily.

"Dane, it was probably spoiled," Graham says. "Eat your sandwich."

"Sure. You're probably right. No big deal," Dane says, giving Matt a toothy grin. He raises his eyebrows and looks over at Graham as he takes a big bite of his sandwich.

119

I know that look, Graham thinks. Nodding at Dane, he takes a bite of his own sandwich and smiles thoughtfully.

In the seat behind them, Jonas gazes out the window and watches the scenery pass by. Before long, having filled his belly with food, Dane is asleep again and snoring with gusto. Mathoni is also asleep and muttering quietly. Graham thumbs through his notepad, rereading the details of Lee's tracks, seemingly oblivious to all the noises in the vehicle.

The sixth man focuses his attention toward the front of the van where John and Liahona Thistleseed have kept up a steady conversation on a range of topics that seem to be mere pleasantries. He studies the profile of the tall man in the passenger seat: strong jaw, bright eyes with heavy brows and deep crow's feet, visible laugh lines at the corners of a full-lipped mouth, straight nose with a slight downward turn at the tip, jet black hair beginning to be shot with silver strands and pulled back into a single braid with the end wrapped in a leather thong.

Jonas considers Thistleseed an exceedingly fine man, as much for his looks as for his intelligence, his bearing, his righteousness, and his ancestry. He knows the Compass (as is the name and the role he now embodies) is the descendent of a great Onondaga leader who was renowned for his oratory skills—a skill the Compass also possesses. The leader was known as *Hiawatha,* a name which means "two river currents flowing together" and is also interpreted throughout historical

120

legends as "he who combs."

Hiawatha has sometimes mistakenly been called *Deganawida* in the Mohawk language, although that was the respectful name given to another man—*Skennenrahawi,* the Great Peacemaker. As does often occur, the two became merged into one person in the legends passed down as tribal oral histories throughout the generations. But Jonas knows differently; he remembers *Deganawida.*

The Great Peacemaker was a prophet who counseled peace among the many warring Iroquois tribes which, at the time, practiced cannibalism. He prophesied of three serpents that would visit the People. The "white serpent" would come as a friend to the lands, only to deceive them later. Then, a "red serpent" would make war against the "white serpent."

In time, a Mohawk boy with a great power would be born into "the land of the hilly country." Because *Deganawida* had a severe speech impediment, it was difficult for him to spread his message of peace. The young Mohawk man would become his voice. He would speak eloquently to the People, whose were plentiful as the blades of grass. His words would be heard by all, and they would make him their chosen leader.

After a season, a "black serpent" would come and defeat both the "white serpent" and the "red serpent." According to *Deganawidah's* prophecy, all three "serpents" would be blinded by a white light many times brighter than the sun. This would only happen once the People gathered under the elm tree and became humble.

"I will be that light," *Deganawidah* proclaimed.

The words of The Great Peacemaker and *Hiawatha* pierced the hearts of the People. The two planted a Tree of Peace at Onondaga Lake to proclaim the Great Binding Law of their founding of the *Haudenosaunee*—the Iroquois Confederacy.

That Mohawk boy known as *Hiawatha* was a direct descendent of Jonas, the unseen sixth passenger in the vehicle.

* * *

On the same highway, many miles back, another unseen passenger waited in the vehicle while the driver took a stretch break. Jim watched carefully as Doctor walked slowly along the grassy shoulder of the road, stooping occasionally to pick colorful wildflowers. Assessing every car that passed, Jim was on the lookout for any that hinted at slowing down and pulling over. He was wary, and for good reason.

Covetress was always near. Wherever they went, she seemed to find them. She was adept at disguises. Everywhere she appeared, she took on a different look. Not only could she change her hair color and style at will, she seemed to be able to reconfigure her features and her bone structure.

Jim knew eye color could be altered with the use of colored contact lenses, but facial shape was a different matter. *Covetress* presented first with a squared jawline, one time with higher cheekbones, another time with smaller ears and

122

attached earlobes, and once with epicanthic eyelid folds which could not have been contrived. Even her skin color was subject to change. He had seen her pale, tan, sallow, freckled, brown, and black—all without the use of cosmetics. She could be tall or short; heavy or thin; ultra-feminine or androgynous. The two things that never varied: she had a recognizable laugh that sent chills up Jim's spine; and she always beheld Doctor with a rapacious glare, as though she wanted to devour him.

Jim was convinced she was not entirely human. In all probability, she was being controlled by an unearthly being— one of the rebellious spirits who had been cast out of Heaven without the privilege of ever being given a tangible body. He shuddered involuntarily. Over the years, he and the others had participated in battles with supernaturals, with possessed innocents, and with some individuals who were truly evil incarnate. Wicked inhuman entities were so jealous of humans.

Though Jim took comfort in the knowledge that the adversary had no power over him and his companions, the battles they were forced to fight were unsettling and often horrific. It was not a duty they took lightly, as each human soul was precious to the Father—even those who went astray—and the battles often resulted in the loss of innocent mortal life.

Jim had known unsuspecting people who unwittingly allowed the evil hosts to enter their minds and souls and eventually inhabit their bodies. The gullible ones were the most heartbreaking to battle, for they were once good people who were led astray by seemingly benign influences: strong drink, mood enhancers, pleasures of the flesh. They were easy targets for the evil ones. Society in these times encouraged doing what felt good…even if it was bad. *No,* he thought, *not just in these times. It was like that in the past, too.*

The Romans tortured and massacred Christians by using them as bait for lions and as practice dummies for gladiators. The Aztecs murdered countless people and utilized their heads as balls in games of hoops. Favoring boys over girls, people in some Asian cultures stuck pins and needles into their undesired infant's heads to bring about their deaths. Humans from all parts of the world were bought and sold as slaves, chattel, playthings. No culture was without its evils, and Jim had been among nearly every culture on the planet.

But each culture was equally blessed with souls worth saving and souls who saved others: empaths, missionaries, parents, siblings, saints, medical practitioners, animal lovers, counselors, ministers, teachers, caregivers, compassionate service providers, warriors and champions, those with kind spirits. He had known them all, and he loved them all.

Jim loved Dr. Fisher. He agonized over the influence that gambling held over the man because he recognized Doctor as one of the saviors. Doctor's hands were meant to heal, not pull a metal lever on a soulless machine that dispensed coins on a whim. Lifegiving power had been bestowed into Jackson Fisher's hands. It was a tremendous gift, and it held tremendous responsibility. Doctor had taken an oath, but the covenants he made were hidden from his heart every bit as much as Jim was hidden from his sight.

Jim's charge was to lead Doctor to a place where he would once again realize his destiny, and where he could be given his own healing. Doctor needed saving because there were those that Doctor needed to save. And one of those belonged to Jim. *My posterity,* Jim thought. *My gift from God.*

CHAPTER ELEVEN
<u>ROAD TRIP</u>

THE RHYTHMIC THUMPING OF THE TIRES over the macadam eventually lulls Jonas to sleep, and he loses himself in a dream. He is within a water vessel, and the waves echo the motion of the van along the highway. He is bound for the promised land.

As is the stuff of dreams, he moves forward and backward in time, ultimately finding he is in the past. He sees his ancestor, Nephi, building a great ship, but not in the manner of men at that time, and without the usual tools used for shipbuilding. The Lord has provided ore to smelt new tools and instructs Nephi in the design of the vessel so it will make the long journey across the ocean.

In his trancelike state, Jonas can clearly see his uncles mocking Nephi. They come toward their brother and try to fight with him, but as soon as they touch him, they are propelled backward as though electrocuted.

Jonas twitches, but thankfully, he makes no noise. The scene shifts onward and becomes the land of that distant shore where his ancestors settled. Jonas is a small child helping his own father construct tools from the native resources. It is a good life, and he is a happy little boy.

Suddenly, he finds himself as a young man. Mathoni stands beside him with his wife, a lovely Ethiopian girl with skin like a starless night. She has also come by ship with many of her people. Her name is Sakhele, and she is great with child. Mathoni rubs her swollen belly affectionately, and she runs her strong fingers through his curly black hair. She grasps it and pulls his face in for a kiss, oblivious to Jonas.

Jonas regards his own wife Sarha as she squats down to wipe the nose of his youngest son. The child twists his face in a vigorous attempt to elude her cloth. He snatches the swatch from her hand and runs away laughing with his mother in pursuit. Jonas watches them taking turns chasing one another, and he sighs as he remembers their games. It has been many, many years, but he reminisces of Sarha often.

His reverie shifts again. He observes himself standing within a group of men—Nephites, Jaredites, and Lamanites—who surround a visitor from the heavens. The man's name is Jesus, and Jonas is one of his 12 followers in this land. Among the others he notices his father Nephi and his uncle Timothy, who was raised from the dead. He can make out Kumen and his son Kumenonhi, Mathoni and his son Mathonihah. Also present are his friends Shemnon, Jeremiah, Zedekiah, Isaiah, and the other Jonas. The Redeemer is about to leave this world.

"What is it that you desire of me, after I am gone to the Father?" Jesus asks them.

Jonas watches as, one by one, the disciples respond.

"We desire that after we have lived to the age of old men, and the ministry you called us to has come to an end, that we may speedily come to you in your Kingdom," they say.

"Blessed are you because of your desire; therefore, after you are seventy-two years old, you shall come to me in my Kingdom and shall find rest," the Lord says.

Jonas and his closest companions Shemnon and Mathoni stand apart, regarding each other uneasily.

"What shall I do unto you when I am gone?" the Holy One asks them.

Jonas feels sorrow, as do the other two, for they are afraid to speak their hearts. But the man called Jesus knows their thoughts, and he blesses them for their desire.

"You three shall never endure the agonies of the flesh nor the pain of death, but you will be transfigured instantly when I return in glory. You shall have much joy in my service as you go among the world and preach my message," he says.

Jonas stands humbly awed as his master reaches forward with his hand. When his finger touches him on the chest, Jonas is immediately taken to a place of unspeakable beauty. His body is changed into something more, something different, and he finds himself in the presence of God. Jonas feels a joy like he has never known.

Just as suddenly, he is thrust back into the present. This time, he does jerk, and his eyes fly open. He sees Mathoni staring at him. Matt kicks the back of Graham's seat quickly.

"Oh, sorry Graham. I was having a wild dream. Didn't mean to kick you," Matt says.

"That's not a problem, Matt. I imagine you're a bit uncomfortable back there. I can't get settled either," Graham says, flexing his shoulders and hips in an attempt to find just a bit more room.

"Hey, John," Matt calls. "Graham and I need to walk for a few minutes. Can you pull over again?"

John obliges by veering over to the roadside where everyone happily disembarks.

"Are we there yet?" Dane groans.

"Getting close," John responds, "but you may want to visit the trees again. I'm probably not stopping anymore until we get to Syracuse."

"I'll join you," Graham says, clapping his hand on Dane's back, "but stay upwind, ok?"

"Look who's talking," Dane says. "I'm the one who smells everything."

Lee, John, and Matt walk to the back of the van and grab more drinks and snacks. Lee is glad he stowed the candies he purchased for his family in his suitcase. Otherwise, with the appetites of this crew, there would be none left.

Meanwhile, behind the tree line, Graham and Dane finish their business, but they do not leave the cover of the woods right away.

"Dane, you gave me look awhile back. What was that about?" Graham asks.

"Ummm. Oh yeah. The burger," Dane says.

"Nobody had a burger, Dane," Graham sighs.

"Oh contraire! Somebody had a burger. I got a good whiff of it. Two all-beef patties, special sauce, lettuce, cheese, pickles, onions, on a sesame seed bun," Dane intones.

"McDonald's was ages ago, Dane. Matt said he threw his burger out. You must've picked up the lingering aroma inside the van," Graham suggests.

"I sniffed a Big Mac, all right. I know my fast food. But I detected it second-hand…from the mouth of somebody who had just eaten it," Dane insists.

"So, Matt lied. He ate his hamburger and didn't throw it away like he said," Graham says.

"Nope. I did not smell burger on *his* breath. But I did smell burger on *somebody's* breath," Dane says petulantly.

"Dane, I did *not* eat a burger," Graham growls. "I had a ham and cheese sandwich, just like you, man."

"Dude. Did I say *you* ate a burger? I did *not*. But *somebody* ate a burger, and it wasn't Matt. I'm just telling you.

130

I smelled a recently-eaten fully-loaded cheeseburger," Dane argues, "and furthermore, *somebody* whizzed beside the van."

"What? Are you sure your smeller is working right?" Graham laughs. "I promise you, nobody peed out there by the road. Except for you, all of us were looking at the *Liahona*."

"Just telling you, dude. Something weird going on around here," Dane says.

"OK, Dane. I believe you, but I can't explain it. For the record, I've heard some strange noises behind me. Matt talks in his sleep and kicks my seat all the time. It's almost like he's trying to tick me off by making a ruckus and disturbing me," Graham complains.

"What's he say?" Dane asks.

"When he talks in his sleep? Mumbles mostly. Some isolated words here and there. I did hear him say something odd, though. '*Isa. Naja.*' I heard that once," Graham says, imitating Matt's voice perfectly.

"Is that Hebrew again?" Dane asks.

"Not any Hebrew I've ever heard. Then he said, '*Isa be kanuring. Isa ben kanuring.*' He said that twice," Graham says, "and that's not Hebrew either."

"What do you think it is?" Dane asks.

"I'm not totally sure what it means, but from the sound of the dialect, I'd say it's more like what Jubal's wife and brother speak. Maybe some African language?" Graham says.

Their conversation is interrupted by a rustling in the

grass. Graham looks up to see Lee coming around the tree line.

"Gentlemen, have you finished your business in the bushes?" he asks, giving them both "the look."

"Oh, sure thing, Lee. We were just talking about..." Graham says.

"...about stuff. You know. Stuff," Dane pipes in.

"Wonderful. Can we get back on the road now, or do you have more 'stuff' to discuss?" Lee asks.

"Nah. We're good," Dane says with a forced smile.

"Yes, I apologize, Lee. It just felt so good to get out of that constricting seat," Graham says.

"I am sorry, Graham. You are a big man. I know you must be terribly inconvenienced with your long legs. Shall I take the back seat?" Lee asks, genuinely sympathetic.

"Thank you, Lee, but I can endure for a while longer. We're almost to Syracuse, aren't we? Let's go," Graham says.

The three men leave the woods and walk to the van. John, Matt, and the unseen sixth passenger are already inside and waiting for them.

"Please forgive us for taking so long," Lee says.

"No apology needed. It's been a long trip," John says.

Dane scoots over to the window, and Graham folds himself back into his own seat. John pulls out onto the road.

"Are we there yet?" Dane jokes.

"Almost, Dane. Only one more hour, if you can make it," John laughs.

"You betcha," Dane says, taking a deep breath.

"Sure thing," Graham says, resting his head against the window, gazing at the ceiling, and listening.

For the next hour, their senses will be on high alert.

*   *   *

The Winnebago RV was no longer on the road. It was stopped and parked in a public rest area. Dr. Fisher replenished his trove of snacks from the vending machines, and after a detour to the rest rooms, he browsed through the newspapers and magazines stacked in the chairs beside the visitor desk. One paper in particular caught his eye. He picked up the New York Times, leaned against the desk, and scanned the article, which was dated months before, in March.

"In May 1990, two Indians died near here in a gun battle between rival Mohawk groups," he read aloud. The piece went on to say that no one had been arrested for the shooting, which was predicated on the issue of casino gambling on the reservation. He read on with more interest.

The editorial stated that in 1990, anti-gambling Mohawks protested for over a month against eight illegal casinos that had opened without state approval. The demonstrators blocked roads and attacked businesses. The protestors included masked Warrior members wearing bandanas across their faces who provided security for the casinos. Pro-gambling Mohawks started the violence by tearing down the roadblocks. Fistfights ensued and escalated

133

into the two fatal shooting deaths, which ultimately led to the closing of all eight of the casinos.

He read further that there was talk of reopening the gambling halls, but many felt it would unleash another stand, inciting pro-gambling Indians to war against their gambling proponents. Apparently, Governor Mario Cuomo was expected to complete an agreement in the coming months that would allow a ten-million-dollar high-stakes casino on the 14,000-acre Mohawk reservation near Syracuse with games like roulette, blackjack, and craps. The projected timeframe was this summer. *This being June, it may already be in the works,* Doctor noted. *Perfect timing!*

Reading further, he discovered that, under the Indian Gaming Regulatory Act of 1988, states were required to allow Indians to operate the same money-making gambling games that charities and other nonprofit groups are allowed to run, including casino-style card and dice games; however, the act did not allow for slot machines.

Doctor considered this news for a moment. *No slot machines? What's the point?* he thought. He needed to revise his plan. But since he was so close, he decided to visit the *Akwesasne* Mohawk land in New York, just to have a look-see, and then maybe cross the border into Canada.

"Excuse me, but can you tell me how to get to the *Akwesasne* reservation?" he asked the restroom attendant.

"Got a map right here, sir," the man said, offering

Doctor a folded pamphlet. "What you going there for?"

"Oh, I just wanted to visit. There's supposed to be a casino there, I think," Doctor said.

"No, sir. You're thinking of the Oneida casino. Governor made a deal with the Oneida Indians. The *Turning-Stone Casino Resort*. It ain't finished being built. Mohawks are still in negotiations for their casino permit, but they ain't been granted federal approval yet," the man said.

"Hm. Interesting. Well, I guess I'll just visit whatever they have up there. Perhaps I'll go see Niagara Falls. Thanks for your help," Doctor said, handing the man a $20 tip.

"God bless you, sir. I hope you find what you're looking for," the man said.

"Yes. So do I," Doctor said. It had been a few days since he fed a one-armed bandit, and he was getting antsy. Turning on his heel, he made his way back to the RV, his ever-present unseen traveling companion close on his heels.

CHAPTER TWELVE
<u>UPSTATE NEW YORK</u>

DESPITE HIS TREPIDATION at being in New York, Dane finds the northern part of the state extremely beautiful, even idyllic. It is exactly as pictured on television, with lush forests, green rolling hills, and wildflowers of all colors. The city of Syracuse, however, gives him flashbacks of New York City, which he has dubbed "the rotten apple." He has determined there will be no walking sojourns outside the hotel like they enjoyed in the quaint setting at Gatlinburg.

Once again, John Revell, with his abundant monetary resources, has provided lavish accommodations for them. The Marriott Syracuse Downtown, a grand refurbishment of an historic building, is impeccably decorated and meticulously clean. The building itself resembles a gigantic uppercase letter "E" laid on its side, covered in rose-colored brick and scores of gleaming rectangular windows.

The room booked for the Trackers is similar to the one they enjoyed at the Opryland Hotel with two plush queen-sized beds and a large writing desk, but with two oversized leather club chairs and a white leather sofa which opens to an equally plush queen-sized bed. At 450 square feet, it is significantly larger than the other rooms in which they've stayed, and it includes special access to the private M Club Lounge and sitting area which overlooks the hotel lobby and at which they may take their meals. Dane decides that upstate New York—inside the hotel, at least—might work out after all.

The two young men are particularly excited that the lounge offers a snack bar with an assortment of hors d'oeuvres and beverages. Dropping their bags and staking claims to the pair of beds, they excuse themselves to take advantage of the food spread, leaving Lee the pull-out bed for his sleeping space. He takes the opportunity to stretch out on the buttery soft, cool unopened couch and bask in the quiet before his companions return from their snack fest.

In an identical room down the hall, John and Jonas claim the beds. Matt, who is somewhat smaller than the other two, is perfectly happy to take the convertible sofa. Jonas is relieved that he is finally able to speak and move about freely without fear of being seen or heard.

"When the Lord said we would suffer no physical pain, he must have forgotten about the small things like cramped muscles and indigestion," Jonas says.

"Work it out, brother," Matt says, "you're going to have to stay hidden for a while yet until we can isolate Dr. Fisher and make sure he is safe from the woman. Then we will be able to allow the Trackers to see you and Shemnon."

"Is there word from Shemnon, John?" Jonas asks.

"I've had no message from him for some time," John says, looking at his cellular phone, "but I have a sense that he is not far behind us. He will contact us whenever they make a stop, as soon as he can safely get to a telephone."

"Well, I don't know about you two, but I am going to take a long, hot shower. If you go to the lounge, will you bring back some food?" Jonas says.

"I have a sneaking suspicion Liahona's young friends are already wolfing down the hors d'oeuvres, but they'll undoubtedly have plenty of room left for dinner in an hour or so. When we leave, why don't you just go ahead and order room service, Jonas? The Trackers won't be coming to our room, so you'll be safe. Have room service leave the tray outside the door, as usual," John says.

"All right. By the way, I am so delighted to meet my heir," Jonas says. "He's a magnificent man."

"That he is, my friend. That he is," John agrees as he dials Lee's room.

Lee answers the phone and listens as John lays out plans to meet for dinner in the M Club Lounge. After hanging up, Lee decides to call home. Wren answers the phone on the second ring.

"Is that you, my little bird?" Lee asks.

"Of course, it's me, silly. Who were you expecting?" Wren twitters.

"I was expecting any member of our offspring, but I was hoping for you," he says.

"Believe it or not, I am home alone. Everyone else has gone to the movies in town. Sali Mata and Arfang have never experienced much, and the kids are having a blast introducing them to American pastimes," Wren says.

"How are things with our new family members? I did not have much time to get acquainted before I was summoned on this journey," Lee says.

"Things are...OK. It's an adjustment. Jubal and Sali Mata have taken up residence in Shine's cottage. I wanted them to have privacy, so Arfang is rooming with Kenny. They are thick as thieves, those two. They chatter all day and night in French, and now Kenny's already speaking Mandinka. It boggles my mind that he can learn all these different languages so quickly," Wren says.

"It is his gift, my bird—that and his mind-link with Luna. Speaking of Luna and tracking gifts, have there been any developments of which I need to be aware?" Lee says.

Wren is silent on the line.

"Wren? Is there something I need to know?" Lee asks.

139

"Nothing as far as tracking is concerned. But there is a...a problem...with Sali Mata, dear." she says.

"What sort of problem?" Lee asks.

"I don't know how to say this except to just say it," Wren admits with a heavy sigh, "Sali Mata is unable to have a physical relationship with Bill." Her voice breaks.

"Oh? Why is that? Does she not love him?" Lee asks.

"Oh, no. It's not that. The two are as madly in love as any couple I have ever seen. It is a...a physical problem. Bill wanted to discuss it with you, but since you were gone, he told me. I know he was embarrassed discussing something this intimate with his mother, though. Liahona, his Sali Mata has been damaged," Wren says.

"Damaged? In what way?" Lee asks in alarm.

"In parts of Africa, like in Sali Mata's village, female children are...they're...it's...it's part of their culture...a sexual thing that is...is forced upon the women," Wren stammers, "and it was done when she was a very small girl."

Lee pales. "Wren, are you saying she was molested? Was she raped?" he asks.

"No, dear. She was...altered. Her female parts were cut," Wren chokes out.

"She has been intentionally mutilated," Lee whispers.

Wren lets out a ragged breath. "Yes, dear. She has. Bill is distraught, and we've spoken to several doctors. It's severe, Lee. The doctors aren't sure they can repair the damage." She breaks down into sobs.

"No, no, little bird. Please, do not despair. I think I have some clarity at last about this quest I have undertaken. We are on the track of a special plastic surgeon who I feel is meant to help Sali Mata. Yes, I am certain of it. Oh, my darling Wren," he commiserates, "that poor girl has recently lost her entire family. She needs your strength as a mother, and I know you can provide that to her. I would ask you not to tell any of the others, though, until we have successfully rescued this doctor from the dangers he currently faces. Have faith, Wren. The Lord has never failed us. This is but another trial we must overcome in our earthly lives."

"I knew you would have the answer. You always do. Please take care, my love, and find that doctor quickly. So...I should say nothing to Jubal?" she asks.

Lee thinks for a few moments before he responds. "I think you *must* tell Jubal in order to put his mind at ease, but please impress upon him the need to keep this knowledge from Sali Mata, the other children, and even the young Trackers there in Florida," Lee says.

"What about Kenny?" Wren asks.

Lee shakes his head knowingly. "I am quite sure Luna has already told our son something is wrong with Sali Mata. I hope she has not gone into detail. Chenaniah is still much too young to have that picture in his mind. Inform him it is imperative that he keep it to himself and let him know we are

141

going to find help for her. Ah, I hear Dane and Graham outside. I must go, little bird. I love you dearly," he says.

"And I, you, Liahona" she responds before hanging up the phone.

Lee pulls open the door to the room and nearly collides with Graham. Dane, bent over at the waist, grins up at him.

"Whoa! You snatched my key card, Hona," Dane says.

"My apologies, Dane. I am just leaving. John has called for us to meet him in the lounge for dinner. I presume you two have already eaten and will not be joining us," Lee says.

Graham plucks the card from the slot in the door and makes an about-face. "No, no. I think we still have plenty of room for dinner. We'll go with you," he says.

"I'm in," Dane confirms, grabbing the card from Graham and following behind Lee.

Lee is grateful that neither Dane nor Graham notice the soberness of his expression. When the time is right, he will let them know about Sali Mata's condition, but before then, he plans to get John Revell alone and confront him.

* * *

Farther upstate near the border between New York and Canada, another confrontation had been planned. The woman waited there patiently. She was the one Shemnon called *Covetress* and Lee identified in his track as a she-jackal, but she had her own name: *Azaneem.* She did not, however, have her own body. She survived by inhabiting a human host until

142

its body wore out. Then, she moved on to hijack another unsuspecting mortal. The woman she possessed now was once called Carla Horn, but it had been a long time since Carla last surfaced. Most likely, she would never surface again.

Azaneem reclined her car seat and stared at the ceiling. Her hair was dark black and hung straight down her back—Carla's original color and cut. Her face was tan, with high cheekbones, dark eyes, and a straight, slightly hooked nose. She pushed the sides of her hair behind her ears and relaxed against the headrest. She could remain in this position all night, for she rarely slept anymore.

The entity had been residing in Carla's body for so long it was conditioned to surviving with very little sleep or nourishment. Whenever *Azaneem* noticed her host beginning to deteriorate, she found shelter and obtained renewal by sleeping for several days at a time and by eating huge amounts of food, which mainly consisted of very rare or raw proteins.

She had been pursuing Dr. Jackson Fisher since before he left the medical convention and embarked on his gambling spree. *Azaneem* did not covet the money; she coveted the man.

Dr. Fisher had a mission in life of which he had no knowledge. But *Azaneem* knew his purpose, and it was imperative that he not be allowed to return to his practice. Her original plan involved seduction, for that was the easiest way to blind a man from following his well-intentioned path. She had seduced many men and derailed their divine purposes.

Thus far, she had attempted to gain control of Dr. Fisher as a cute blond party girl, a chic businesswoman, a brainy college student, an exotic Asian, and a soccer mom. He had resisted her advances on every occasion, but not without help at times from some other human.

She came on too strong in Louisiana, and he had run scared, so she toned it down, but that was also unsuccessful. In Mississippi, she nearly had him, but some fool spilled a bucket of coins at the man's feet and distracted him. And then that cursed child at the Cherokee Indian Reservation had tricked her. *A child!* She almost slipped out of her corporeal form and attacked the urchin, but there were too many people around, and there was a powerful opposing force that she couldn't readily identify.

She planned to make another attempt at seduction when he arrived at *Akwesasne.* He was already in upstate New York and would be at the reservation tomorrow. She would play the part of a Mohawk tourist guide, utilizing Carla's original form and heritage. The unsuspecting doctor would join the ranks of the men she had wooed and discarded. Like the others she succeeded in diverting, he would be left hopelessly lost, never to meet his potential—provided he lived, that is.

Azaneem took great pleasure in leaving men in despair and ruin, and many succumbed to such remorse and depression that they took their own lives. But *Azaneem* also loved to kill. She was a skillful, cruel assassin. Because she could transform herself at will, she often devolved into the hideous form of the sadistic creature that personified her essence. The very sight of her was terrifying to her prey, even before her sharp teeth and claws ripped their flesh and spilled their blood. She relished their screams for mercy.

This time, I will have him, she vowed.

* * *

Graham and Dane enter their room and are already vying for turns showering and making phone calls home. Matt enters his own room, but Lee stops John with a firm hand on his arm.

"How long have you known about my daughter-in-law's condition?" Lee asks. His voice is low and softly modulated, but his black eyes blaze.

John catches his breath and blinks quickly at the closed door before he turns to face Lee.

"I asked you a question, John Revell. When did you know?" Lee asks.

"Lee. I'm so sorry. I was not altogether sure, but I suspected. It is common practice in the villages of West Africa. I hoped Sali Mata had not been subjected to the procedure, but I was afraid she had been," John admits.

"Why did you not inform me, John?" Lee asks. "Did you not think I should know? My son has married this girl."

"I am aware of that, Lee. I intended to discuss it with you, but then you found the *Liahona*, and we got caught up in this quest, and things just went along," John says shrugging.

"Did the *Liahona* tell you we are to track down this doctor, or is this *you* leaning to *your* own understanding?" Lee says pointedly.

John Revell's eyes widen. He never raises his voice, but his tone is firm as he stands face to face with Lee.

"The *Liahona* merely gives direction, Lee. It does not name people. I received the doctor's name through personal revelation *weeks* ago. I only found out about Jubal and Sali Mata a *few days* ago when I learned one of our missionaries had run off to Senegal and married a village girl. Even then, I didn't realize she had suffered this mutilation. And I had no idea Dr. Fisher would be the very person who could repair the damage. I merely knew that I was instructed to find him and bring him back to Florida. That's how the Lord works. I'm sorry if it seemed like I was deceiving you. I've been operating on faith, just like you have," he explains.

"I do not like being kept in the dark, John. As I told you before, we have left our families and our jobs to complete this quest. I am a faithful, covenant-keeping person. I do my utmost to be honest and true in my dealings with my fellow man. I presume my friends will do the same," Lee says. He is fighting to control his emotions, but his voice betrays him.

"You are right, of course. I'm ashamed that I didn't tell you. I truly am. I hope you can forgive me," John states, taking a step back and putting some space between them.

146

"That is a given, John. I am also a forgiving man. But from this moment forward, I expect the truth from you. Can you do that?" Lee asks.

"Yes. Yes. I will be up front with you," John replies.

"Very well. Be honest with me about Matt," Lee says.

"Matt is my friend...has been my friend for years. I didn't just happen to run into him in Tennessee. We arranged to be there at the same time. He also received revelation about Dr. Fisher and this quest. We need Matt because he has a particular skill set that may come into play," John says.

"What would that be?" Lee asks.

"Matt is a holistic healer. We have reason to believe this she-jackal you spoke of in your track intends to harm Dr. Fisher. If that should happen, Matt's healing ability will be invaluable. Lee, I cannot stress enough the importance of finding and safeguarding Dr. Fisher. Your daughter-in-law is not the only person who needs his surgical expertise. There are others we don't even know about yet. We have to find and protect this doctor no matter what," John says.

"For the sake of my son's wife, I hope he is everything you believe him to be. Is there anything else I need to know that you have not yet told me?" Lee asks calmly.

"I already told you about the man named Jim. There is another man named Joe who is also helping us locate the doctor. He's a big brawny guy like Graham. We will need his great physical strength if Dr. Fisher is placed in any danger of bodily harm. You'll probably see Joe and Jim before too long. Other than that, there's nothing else I can tell you. So, are we OK?" John says tentatively.

"Thank you, John. I hated to confront you, but the news from home was upsetting," Lee says. "I regret that I lost control. It is not like me."

"I understand completely, my friend. We are all under considerable pressure. I apologize as well for getting in your face," John says dropping his chin down to his chest.

"Of course. If you do not mind, I would rather Dane and Graham not know about Sali Mata just yet. I prefer to tell them myself," Lee says.

"Absolutely," John says, offering his open hand.

Lee grasps John's hand and shakes it solemnly. Their eyes meet, and they exchange a quick nod before John disappears into his hotel room.

Lee walks down the hall and stands in front of his room. He can hear Dane and Graham murmuring inside. He places his hands flat against the door frame and closes his eyes, praying silently. Before he inserts his key card into the slot, he wipes away the tears which have escaped his eyes. And then, he goes inside to get some well-needed rest.

CHAPTER THIRTEEN
<u>AKWESASNE</u>

"COME IN! HI! HELLO! HOW ARE YOU? *Tasatáweiat! Kwe!
Shé:kon! Skennenkó:wa ken?* Welcome to the *Akwesasne*
Cultural Center. *Iakentiohkowá:nen nón:wa ken' í:iens.* My
name is Ms. Horn. *Ms. Horn ióntiats.* There are a lot of people
here today, and I will be your guide," the pretty woman chirped.

"The Mohawk Nation straddles the international border
between the United States and Canada along both banks of the
St. Lawrence River, or *wa'thiátera'ne*, which we say is the place
'where those two met each other.' Although we are referred to as
Mohawk, we prefer to be called by our correct name,
Kanien'kehá:ka, which means 'People of the Flint Nation.' The
name of this territory is *Akwesasne*, which means 'land where
the partridge drums.' It refers to the rich wildlife which inhabits
this area.

"In the United States, the *Akwesasne* territory is federally recognized as the St. Regis Mohawk Reservation. It is flanked by the New York state towns of Fort Covington, Bombay, and Massena and includes many of the islands in the St. Lawrence River, as well as the communities of Raquette Point, Frogtown, and Hogansburg," the tour guide said.

Dr. Fisher listened with interest, enjoying the narrative as much as the attractive woman conducting the tour. She was in her mid-to-late forties, dressed in khaki pants, tan shirt, and sensible walking boots. A willowy woman of Mohawk descent with lustrous ebony hair that fanned out over her shoulders, she smiled often and engaged well with the assembled tourists.

Doctor's tagalong Jim scrutinized her with narrowed eyes, but she didn't seem to be singling Doctor out, so he continued scanning the crowd, always on the lookout for *Covetress,* the she-jackal.

"Early indigenous Iroquoian-speaking people settled around the Great Lakes area and cultivated *o'nenste,* which is maize or corn as most people know it, along with squash and beans, which we still call 'the three sisters.' We caught *kvja'ko'wa,* or big fish, in the river and hunted all types of game. The Mohawk built villages along the fertile river valley and engaged in fur trading, war parties, and the ransom of captives from New England settlements. Those English women and children that were not ransomed were adopted into the tribe," she said, "and if you'll follow me, we'll take a look

150

at where they lived."

The *Akwesasne* Cultural Center was always a popular attraction, and there were about 25 people in this early morning group. Because of his height, striking looks, and white hair, Dr. Fisher naturally stood out. Several of the women, including the guide, seemed to be rather taken with him. He was flattered, but he didn't want to appear overly interested. They entered a glass door and funneled into a long, narrow building.

"This wooden structure is a house, called a *kanónhsa*, or a longhouse. It is constructed of poles covered with rectangular slabs of bark and has a rounded roof, as you can see. Longhouses were built next to the streams and rivers and housed multiple families who stored their food and belongings inside. A longhouse could hold as many as 20 families, so having access to clean water was a necessity. These homes were about ten or 12 feet wide and often 100 feet long. Of course, they didn't have a glass door, or *kanhoha*, but we need it to keep out critters and vagrants," she remarked. Several people tittered at her charming delivery.

"In the summertime, especially on warm days like today, the men went shirtless with just breechcloths and hide moccasins, called *ahtahkwa'ón:we*. The women were a little more covered up with tunics or wraparound shirts over short leggings, but they were still a bit skimpy. In the winter, they kept warm with shirts, robes, or jackets made of animal hides with the fur intact over leggings," she said.

The doctor imagined the guide in the clothing she described, and he beamed at her. She graced him with a beautiful smile in return as the crowd walked along through the longhouse and viewed the representative items within. Standing directly behind Doctor with people pressed on either side, Jim did not see the flirtatious look pass between Dr. Fisher and the tour guide.

"The men wore feathered headdresses. Every tribe had an entirely different configuration of colors and feathers. The *Kanien'kehá:ka* traditionally wore three eagle feathers on the top of their headdresses. The women wore lovely beaded tiaras. The ladies all had long hair that was only cut if they were in mourning, but the men had that hairstyle that came to be known as the 'Mohawk.' The sides were removed, leaving a narrow row on the top from front to back. Grease was applied to make it stick up. And they didn't shave the hair, folks. They plucked it out, hair by hair. Ouch!" she playfully rubbed her head, and the guests chuckled with her.

"The *Kanien'kehá:ka* were skilled artists. We are still known for beadwork and handcrafted porcupine quill jewelry. Our artists also carve ornate masks that are used in religious ceremonies, but these masks are never sold. We do, however, have a wonderful assortment of jewelry and tiaras for sale in our gift shop, which is right through here. You should make a visit. *Asenatara'*. Thank you for your attention, and please enjoy the rest of your tour in our *Akwesasne* Library and

152

Cultural Center. Goodbye. *Ó:nen,*" she said as she directed the tourists, including Jim, hidden within the crowd, through the door in the end of the longhouse and locked it behind them.

Dr. Fisher had hung back, hoping to talk with her. He was pleasantly surprised when he saw her turn away from the locked door and walk towards him.

"How did I do?" she asked.

"Very well. I enjoyed your presentation very much," he said. "Have you been doing this long?"

"Not really. This is actually my first summer as a tour guide. Are you very interested in our Mohawk culture?" she asked, walking briskly toward the other end of the longhouse.

"Ah, well, I could be more interested if I had someone like you to guide me," he responded as he followed her out of the building.

"I have about an hour before my next tour. Would you like to see some of the sights that are off the beaten path? I can show you, if you'd like," she said with a bright smile. She quickly locked the door behind them.

"Well, yes. That sounds fun," he said.

"Great! Hurry up. Follow me. My name's Carla, by the way," she said extending her hand.

"I'm Jackson. Good to meet you," he said taking her offered hand.

"You too, Jackson. Let's scoot over this way," she said, hurriedly leading him away from the cultural center and down an unbeaten path toward the St. Regis River. "Did you know they're going to build a casino nearby?"

"Are they, now?" he said with interest.

"Yes. No slot machines though. I wish they'd have slots. I like to pull that bandit's arm," she teased.

"I'm partial to the one-armed bandit myself," he said.

"Come on. I'll show you where they've staked it all out. Since it's Saturday, I don't think they're working. We'll have the whole site to ourselves," Carla said.

"That sounds like a plan to me," the doctor responded. He didn't realize until just that moment she had not let go of his hand.

By the time Shemnon frantically maneuvered through the throng of tourists and ran out of the *Akwesasne* Cultural Center, Dr. Jackson Fisher and Ms. Carla Horn had descended the hill and were completely out of sight.

* * *

Checking out of the Marriott Downtown Syracuse after a delicious breakfast in the M Club Lounge, the Trackers and their traveling companions climb into the van and drive toward the *Akwesasne* territory. They make good time and anticipate arrival in less than one hour.

Lee is particularly anxious to visit the St. Regis Mohawk Reservation, not just because of his position as a history professor at Florida State University, but because his ancestors were Mohawk. He is proud of his lineage, and he plans to bring back some Native wares, photographs, and historical books so his family can learn more about their ancestors. He especially wants to find a *Kanien'kéha* language book for Chenaniah's birthday next month.

"Did you know that I am a direct descendent of *Hiawatha*?" he asks John.

"Is that right? That's quite a heritage, Lee," John says with a genuine smile.

After last night's confrontation, all is forgiven, and the two men are back on friendly terms.

"Please don't ask him to tell the story," Dane warns.

Lee scowls at Dane, which causes Graham to snort and snicker. "I learned my lesson already," he says.

"Hmph. Is that so? Well, gentlemen, I will relate some things about the *Kanien'kehá:ka* you may not have heard before. *Kanien'kehá:ka* means 'people of the flint' and is in reference to the skill of flint knapping, of which my people were quite well versed. In the early- to mid-16th century, the Great Peacemaker *Deganawida* and my ancestor *Hiawatha* founded the Iroquois Confederacy and brought peace to the warring Iroquois tribes.

"The Mohawk men were hunters, traders, warriors, and chiefs. Chiefs made trade agreements and decisions about war. The women farmed, took care of the family, made all decision regarding land and property, and, interestingly, were the only ones who could vote on who would be chief.

"After contact with Europeans such as the French and Dutch, the Mohawk tribe contracted their diseases. A smallpox epidemic proved deadly and greatly reduced the population. In the 18th century, many of the remaining Mohawk moved into Southeastern Canada on the other side of the St. Lawrence River. Today, the tribe resides throughout upstate New York and in Canada, both on and off reservations.

"In the early 20th century, Mohawk men were well known for their participation in the construction of the George Washington Bridge and the Empire State Building because they had no fear of heights. In fact, it was a sign of bravery to perform that type of risky work, so, of course, the Mohawk men stepped up to the challenge.

"The history of my people, important events, and tribal treaties were recorded on wampum belts. These belts were mnemonic devices in the absence of a written language. They were made up of patterns of colored beads, and each color had a specific meaning, which helped promote memory recall. Did you know that the government separated children from their homes and families in an effort to keep them from learning their own language or observing their long-held traditions," Lee reports.

"Mommy, please, make him stop," Dane whines.

Everyone in the vehicle, including Lee, chortles and hoots at Dane's remark.

"Thank goodness! I wondered if you were ever going

to stop me, Dane. I was running out of things to say," Lee says.

"What? You suckered me again?" Dane says.

"Do not think I am unaware of how you all feel about my stories," Lee says with a pinched expression.

"No, Hona. We love your stories…just not so many… and not so long," Dane explains.

Graham makes the fish-hook-in-the-mouth gesture again, and everyone cackles—Dane included.

Their boisterous kidding is cut short by a shrill ringing from the mobile phone in John's shirt pocket. He pulls the antenna up and puts the phone to his ear, and then he veers off the road and parks the van on the shoulder. His face goes white as he listens.

"How did that happen?" he asks.

"John? Is it Shemnon?" Matt asks from the back seat.

John nods. "We're on the way. Maybe 20, 30 minutes out. Keep looking. We'll find you," he directs. He is trembling.

"John? What's happened?" Matt says.

"It's Jackson Fisher. Shemnon lost sight of him. She was there. She's got him," John says. He pulls the van back onto the road and fishtails as he jams on the accelerator.

"The jackal? She has Dr. Fisher?" Lee asks.

John nods, unable to speak as he concentrates on getting to *Akwesasne* Cultural Center as quickly as possible.

Graham and Dane exchange puzzled looks. "Who is Shemnon?" Graham says quietly. Dane shrugs.

"Shemnon is our companion. He's the one we call Jim," Matt responds. "He has been traveling with the doctor since he began his gambling spree in Las Vegas."

The Trackers peer at Matt in the back seat.

"The private investigator?" Dane says puzzled.

"What do you mean *traveling with* him? I thought he was *tailing* him," Graham asks.

"He's been riding in Dr. Fisher's motorhome, same as I've been traveling with you guys, except the doctor was unaware of Shemnon's presence," Matt says, distracted.

"What? How is *that* possible?" Dane asks.

"It is possible because he has not wished himself to be seen. Am I correct, John?" Lee says, staring at his friend.

John nods slowly, glancing sidelong at Lee.

"And the man called Joe. He is also unseen unless he wishes to be revealed. Is that right?" Lee says.

Again, John nods slowly.

"What are you talking about, Lee?" Graham asks.

"I am speaking of three men who are not from our century, Graham. Three men who are serving a special mission on earth and who will not die until the Savior returns to earth. Dane, you know the ones of which I speak," Lee says.

"Are you saying Jim, or Shemnon I guess, is one of the three Nephite disciples?" Dane asks.

"I am saying precisely that," Lee says. "It all makes sense now. The *Liahona*. The quest. The adversarial jackal."

"Uh, nah. I don't think so. I've read about them, but I don't think...I mean...of course, they're real...but *we* wouldn't ever meet them," Dane says.

"No? Have you men not witnessed things which are beyond our understanding? Graham, did we not just fight against enemies made of nothing more than sand? Did not monsters from ancient legends threaten to kill us? I was with you, remember?" Lee points out.

"Well, yes. But that was...that was..." Graham says, clutching the turquoise pendant on his necklace.

"That was unbelievable, was it not? But it happened. How can this be any less believable?" Lee reasons.

"Raven told me she drew this jackal woman and that her whole face changes shape. It sounds pretty weird, but I'm thinking Lee may be right about this, Gray," Dane says.

"I don't know, man. This is a lot to take in," Graham says shaking his head.

"Dude. You fought *monsters*, for crying out loud, and you're not believing this? Listen, my wife had twins in the middle of a blizzard, and two pronghorn antelopes carried her up the mountain and put her beneath a tree while she was in labor! That tells me anything's possible," Dane says.

"Wait, wait, wait. Let me wrap my head around this from my own perspective. The languages I heard. I'm guessing one was African. You said, *'Isa Naja'* and *'Isa be kanuring. Isa ben kanuring.'* What was that?" Graham asks Matt.

159

"You're right, Graham. It is African—a Mandinkan dialect. *Jesus come down, Jesus loves you. Jesus loves me'* is the translation," Matt says.

"And I know that wasn't Hebrew you and John were using, that first night, was it? It was Aramaic. How many languages do you speak, Matt?" Graham asks.

"All of them," Matt responds quietly.

"Huh?" Dane says.

"*Ahił danihidzul.*" Matt's eyes seem to twinkle.

Graham's face gets pasty.

"What did he say, Gray?" Dane asks.

"He said, *'we are strong together.'* He said it in perfect Navajo," Graham answers.

"Dude," Dane whispers.

Graham leans forward in his seat. "John Revell are you one of these Nephites?" he asks.

John shakes his head slowly from side to side.

"No? Matt? You are one, aren't you?" Graham asks, turning toward the back seat.

"I am, Graham. My given name is Mathoni, and I am hundreds of years old. Our friend's name is Shemnon, and he is on the same quest we are," Matt says.

"Who's this Joe guy you mentioned, Lee?" Dane asks.

A large man appears beside Mathoni. "I am," he states. "My name is Jonas. I am the third Nephite disciple."

160

CHAPTER FOURTEEN
THE JACKAL

"WHAT'S HAPPENED?" Jackson Fisher moaned. He struggled to be aware, but his mind would not cooperate. He was hurting...badly. He tried to ferret out the location of the discomfort, but he seemed to be aching everywhere. The back of his head throbbed, and when he made the slightest movement, he feared he would vomit. *Concussion,* he realized. *I've suffered a head trauma, and likely bruises and contusions.*

He lay still and tried to open his eyes, but they stung. He squeezed them tightly shut, letting his tears wash out the foreign substance that was obstructing his vision. He detected that telltale coppery smell. *Blood. Blood in my eyes*, he decided. Wrinkling his forehead, he surmised the blood came from a deep scalp laceration.

As he assessed his condition, he became aware of the

severe pain in the palms and backs of his hands. He tried to move his arms, but they were outstretched and held fast. He flexed his fingers and immediately wished he had not. He cried out, and when he did, he heard someone snicker nearby.

"Help me," he called. "I've been in an accident."

"Wrong. This is no accident," the person said.

Doctor tried desperately to sort out the voice. It was familiar, and unfamiliar at the same time. His head pounded.

"Help me, please," he begged. "I've been injured."

"Now that is certainly true," the voice said. "You have been injured, but not nearly enough."

"What?" Doctor asked. "Please, can you help me?" He wasn't sure he had heard correctly. *Did she—yes, it was a she—say I had not been injured enough?*

"I can, but I won't. I rather like you this way," she said.

And then, he knew her. "Carla? Carla, what happened to us? Are you all right?" he asked.

"Carla can't come to the phone right now," she said.

"Please, I can't see you," he implored.

"Oh, no. Too much blood in your eyes? Here, let me wipe it away," she said. Getting down on hands and knees, the woman leaned over his face and examined the blood covering his eyes. Then, she opened her mouth and proceeded to lick it off, smacking her lips when she had finished.

Dr. Fisher flinched and tentatively opened his lids, blinking rapidly, letting his tears wash out the salt from her putrid saliva. He could make out Carla's face peering down at him—albeit a warped, corrupted version of Carla's face. Her once pretty mouth was smeared with red gore.

"Carla?" he whispered, his mind already in denial.

"Told you. Carla's gone away," she said.

"Who...who are you?" he asked.

"My name is *Azaneem*. Isn't that a pretty name? I'm so pleased to meet you. I'd shake your hand, but sadly, your hands are otherwise engaged," she sneered.

"My...hands. What's happened to my hands? I can't move them," he said with a shudder.

"Oh, I wouldn't try that if I were you. Gotta hurt something fierce. If you pull on them, you'll tear them more," the woman said. Her expression was deadpan.

Dr. Fisher gingerly rolled his head to the side so that he could see his right hand in his peripheral vision, and then he did vomit. His hand was anchored to the ground by a long wooden stake. A red surveyor's flag waved obscenely from the top of the pole. He gagged and threw up more bile.

"Now, don't try and look at the other one, Doctor. You'll just get upset. It's the same. A matched pair. Kinda pretty, if you ask me," she mocked.

"Why?" he gasped.

"Why not?" she replied.

"I've done nothing to you, Carla," he said.

"I told you, my name is *Azaneem*. Carla has left the

building," she shouted, spraying foul spittle over his face.

"I'm sorry. *Azaneem*. Clearly, I've upset you in some way. I have plenty of money, if that's what you want. Cash. I have lots of cash. I'll give you all of it. You'll be a rich woman," he said. *She's lost her mind*, he thought. *Play along.*

"Stupid human. I don't want your money. I can have whatever I want just by taking it," she scoffed.

"All right. Then what? Whatever you want, I can give it to you. Just take these things out of my hands and let me go, Car...*Azaneem*. You need never see me again," he petitioned.

The jackal yawned, revealing a mouth full of sharp jagged teeth.

I did not see that, the doctor told himself.

"You're beginning to bore me, Doc. Where's your fight? Where's your spunk? You're like all the others, begging and crying and bargaining as though I care one iota what you think or want," she snarled.

"I'm trying to give you what you want, *Azaneem*, but I don't know what that is," he said, becoming lightheaded as shock began to set in.

"I want you right here, staked to this ground. I want to leave you without your greatest asset—your surgical ability. That's why I've destroyed your hands, don't you see? Don't worry, you can still pull a slot machine lever with your crippled limbs. But you'll never operate on a human body again. *That's* what *I* want," she spat.

"I think you've accomplished that, *Azaneem*. I don't know why you wanted it, but you've won. I'm finished as a surgeon," he said. His tongue felt dry and thick.

"Aren't you interested in *why* I want to ruin you? I'll tell you. You're a renowned plastic surgeon who's worked on countless people, making them flawless. And there are more that you could fix...if you had the chance...but I've taken that away from you. My master doesn't want those people fixed, and I serve him and do his bidding," she said haughtily.

"I see. Your master. So, you're doing this because your master told you to," he said, growing weaker and quieter.

"That's right. But even if he didn't command it, I'd still want to ruin you, Dr. Jackson Fisher, famous plastic surgeon. Why should someone else have a perfect body when *I* can't have one? I have to *steal* bodies. Did you know that? And they always wear out," she said, anger contorting her features.

The jackal jumped astride Fisher's prone form and sat down heavily on his pelvis. He groaned. Her face twisted into an inhuman grotesque mask of the hapless woman she currently possessed. She stretched out her hands, and her fingernails became long sharp talons. Reaching forward and down, she clawed him through his silk shirt from the top of his chest to his waist—right hand, left hand, right hand, left hand.

"They. Always. Wear. Out!" She shrieked. Then, she sprang up and ran screeching and cackling into the nearby woods, leaving Jackson Fisher bleeding from the torso and staked through his hands to the broken ground of the future site of the *Akwesasne* Mohawk Casino Resort.

* * *

John Revell slams the van into park and leaps out the driver's door. He runs into the parking lot and calls to Shemnon, who is hidden beside Dr. Fisher's RV.

"Shemnon, be seen," John demands.

Immediately, Shemnon appears. As the Trackers exit the van, they see John run into the lot, and then they see a man materialize into view before him. Shemnon spots them, along with Mathoni and the now-visible Jonas.

"Are we seen to these men now?" he asks.

"Tell me what happened," John urges, ignoring Shemnon's question.

"*Covetress* took on the form of an Indian tour guide. She was convincing. It was by far her best disguise. She showed little interest in Doctor, so I was fooled. Forgive me, John. I've failed us," Shemnon said sadly.

Instead of being angry, John steps forward and embraces the man, who weeps on his shoulder.

"No, Shemnon. Remain faithful. We have help. These are the Trackers, and, yes, they know who you are. You are all seen," John explains.

Dane lifts his hand. "Uh, hi. I'm Dane Lightfoot. Nice to meet you," he says with an awkward grin.

"I'm Graham Skysong. Likewise," Graham murmurs.

166

"Time for that later, boys. Where have you searched?" Lee asks, taking charge as he always does when tracking.

"The buildings, the grounds, the parking lot. They've vanished. I don't know if she's taken him by foot or by vehicle. They could be miles away by now," Shemnon admits.

"Is this his motorhome?" Lee asks. "Let us go inside."

Shemnon opens the door, and all seven men climb in. Dane pulls the door closed as Lee Thistleseed takes a seat on the sofa. Graham has already pulled out the two notepads from his back pocket. He hands one to John as Dane takes a seat beside Lee.

"Are you going to consult the *Liahona*?" Shemnon asks with interest.

"In a way," Graham says. "We're going to consult *our* Liahona. He is *our* Compass. Everyone be very quiet, please, while we do what we do best." And with that, Lee and Dane begin breathing in sync.

"The healer runs with the she-jackal along a grassy path that twists and turns and descends a hill. The regent saint's water sparkles in the distance. The ancient hunting grounds are scraped and bare, laid fallow by large-mouthed dragons who puff smoke but who are now silent. A boundary of crimson flags wave around the hunting grounds near the crooked body of water. The she-jackal keeps her prey subdued as if in crucifixion. He bleeds. He cries. He awaits us. And the Tracker now comes home," Lee intones.

167

As Dane and Lee both open their eyes, Graham and John are already deciphering the poem.

"They were on foot. Thank the Lord," John says.

"Down a meandering path. Down a hill. Regent saint's water in the distance," Graham says.

"The St. Lawrence River? That's toward Canada," Matt says.

"No, no. Not that one. It's his Southern accent. Not regent's saint...*regis* saint. St. Regis River," John says.

"That's just over the ridge, about five minutes from here," Shemnon shouts.

"Hunting grounds scraped and bare. Smoke puffing dragons. Construction site?" Dane says.

"Yes! 'A boundary of crimson flags wave around the hunting grounds near the crooked body of water.' He said that same thing yesterday. A construction site near the river with surveyor's stakes. Of course," John says, already moving toward the door. "Let's go quickly men."

"He is alive, but she's hurt him. He's bloody. Mathoni, your skills will be crucial," Lee says. His manner is urgent now.

"I know. Crucifixion. I fear his injuries are going to be substantial, and his hands may be damaged," Mathoni says.

"Then you will fix him, Matt," Dane announces.

"And she's gonna be sorry," Graham says, flexing his large fists menacingly as he jumps to the ground.

Jonas reaches out and clamps his hand on Graham's

shoulder. "No, no, my burly friend. Stand down. You may not fight this jackal. None of you may," he says, giving them each a stern look. "That is for us to do."

Dane steps up beside him, clasping the large Bowie knife that the Lightfoot men are famous for wielding. "And why not?" he challenges.

Jonas shrugs and smiles. "Because you are mortal. That's why not," he says, and then he takes off down the hill behind John and Matt.

Dane and Graham quickly catch up, and Lee follows them at his own pace. He knows the three Nephites will do the fighting, but he is anxious to make sure the doctor is going to live. What's more, he must be able to perform surgery, not just for Sali Mata's sake, but for the others that are interwoven in his destiny.

"I smell him," Dane says. "I smell the blood."

"And I hear his labored breathing. He's alive, but he's in serious respiratory distress," Graham says.

"Run faster," Lee urges them.

In a matter of minutes, they see the flags surrounding the construction site. Staked out in the center is the prone body of Jackson Fisher. Matt runs to the doctor and checks his condition while Jonas, John, and Shemnon arrange themselves protectively at his feet and sides. The jackal is nowhere in sight. The Trackers arrive on the scene and stand between the doctor and the river at the doctor's head. The sight of his injured body is ghastly. The damage is undeniably severe.

Dr. Fisher's arms are outstretched, and his hands have been pierced through the palms with the pointed ends of the rough wooden survey stakes. His legs are lying straight, but they have been made immovable with hoops of metal at the ankles and hips.

"Is that...rebar?" Dane asks, not believing what he is seeing. "It's bent completely around him. Eight-foot lengths of steel bars. Graham, nobody just bends rebar!"

Graham cannot take his eyes from the man's torso where deep parallel slashes have oozed blood through his shredded shirt. *What kind of beast would do this?* He wonders.

Mathoni motions to Dane and Graham to help him pull the stakes carefully from the ground. While they determine how to unearth the stakes without inflicting further damage, Lee kneels at the man's head and begins to pray. Dr. Fisher moans as they inadvertently move his hands, but Lee places his palms tenderly against the side of his face and continues praying in a low, singsong voice, soothing him.

Mathoni examines Fisher's hands closely. Grasping the stake securely, he pulls it from the doctor's right hand in one swift motion. Fisher cries out, but Lee continues to calm him. After packing the hole of the open wound with saliva, herbs from his medicine pouch, and damp earth that he digs from the ground, Mathoni moves to the other hand. He repeats the process as tenderly and painlessly as he can, removing the stake and packing the wound.

While he works on the doctor's hands, Dane and Graham struggle to remove the doubled-over rebar from the man's legs. They grab the bar on both sides, and together they pull until they have unearthed all four feet on each side. Casting it aside, they begin pulling the bar from over his hips.

Dane lets go of the rebar and jams his fingers into his nostrils. "Oh Lord. Do you smell that?" He coughs and gags.

"Not my gig, man. What do you smell?" Graham says.

"Putrid rotting flesh. Death warmed over," Dane says, breathing through his mouth.

Then Graham stands upright. "I hear movement in the trees. Something's coming," he says in alarm.

Suddenly, there is an ear-splitting sound as the jackal emerges from the woods. Like a crazed banshee, she runs shrieking toward the party. Dane and Graham promptly squat and lift, tugging on the rebar until it finally comes free, and then they hastily back away behind Lee at Fisher's head.

"Stay there," Mathoni warns. "You must not attempt to engage her. She is deadly. Take solace in whatever you have that brings you comfort."

Graham immediately pulls out the carved turquoise pendant necklace. He cradles it against his heart and thinks of Shinehah and the baby they will soon have. Dane reaches in his back pocket and palms the picture of his twin sons, Buck and Perry, and their beautiful mother Raven. From his side pocket, he pulls a downy goose feather wrapped in colorful embroidery thread. It is a protection token given to him by his mother Fawn, the feather courtesy of her pet goose Emma. He places them against his chest as he pants shallowly, watching the approach of the jackal. Lee, at the head of Dr. Fisher, needs no tokens. He is girded by prayer. Mathoni keeps an eye on them while he continues ministering to his patient.

The jackal stops running and stands weaving from side to side. She spreads her legs wide, bending at the knees, and assumes a battle stance. Her fingers end in sharp claws, and her mouth widens to an improbable size, revealing pointed teeth with prominent canines. She barely resembles a human being. She growls and slobbers as she approaches, her eyes darting from side to side, glaring at the men before her.

Without warning, she howls and rushes forward. John Revell sidesteps just before she reaches him, and Jonas catches her by the hair, snapping her head backwards. He grabs her arm and wrenches it at the shoulder socket, and she lets out a high-pitched wail. Shemnon grabs her other arm and pulls it backward. As the two men hold on, the jackal plants her feet and tries to leap into the air. She is strong, and the men are pulled upward nearly a foot off the ground.

When they regain their footing, Jonas wraps his arms around her from the back, pinning both of her arms to her side. Shemnon slides down and encircles her ankles with his crossed legs while getting a firm grip on her wrists to keep her from slashing either of them with her nails. John stands calmly to the side, nonplussed.

In the meantime, the three Trackers a few feet away are watching different battles taking place.

Dane sees Noah wrestling with a mugger in a pea coat who wields a switchblade. He watches helplessly as Noah's head is jerked back and the mugger reaches forward, hacking through his long black hair. "Whoop, whoop, whoop. I scalped me an Indian. Now I'm gonna scalp the other one," the mugger taunts. Dane's knees grow weak, and he shakily sits down on the ground.

Mathoni extends his arm and touches Dane. "Be at peace, Dane Lightfoot," he purrs. Dane is instantly relaxed.

Graham perceives an abomination composed entirely of swirling white sand and shaped like a huge fat starfish. It is *Yé'iitsoh*—Big Giant Monster. He is horrified to see his precious wife stand up to face the giant. "Shine! Noooo!" he cries. "Stab it in the head! Stab it in the head!" The monster throws its arms forward and closes them around her waist, lifting her off her feet.

Graham starts to move forward, but Mathoni reaches up and grabs his knee, stopping him. "Be at peace, Graham Skysong," he croons. Graham sighs and is still.

Lee looks up and is surprised to find *Tsikonsaseh,* an elder known for her wise counsel, with *Atotarhoh*, an Onondaga leader of great savagery. He is vile to look upon,

173

with a body bent in seven places and snakes growing from his hair. "Don't look at him," Lee cries, "or you will go insane."

Mathoni puts his hand over Lee's. "Be at peace, Liahona Thistleseed," he whispers. At once, Lee is tranquil.

Now, the Trackers see the battle as it truly is. Jonas holds the jackal's arms, and Shemnon secures her legs and hands. John Revell steps up and places his palms against the sides of her face, holding her head immobile.

The jackal spits and bites at him, baring her fearsome teeth in a growl. "*Iák kenh tesahterón:ni?* —Aren't you afraid?" she taunts in Mohawk.

John compresses her face more forcefully.

"Who are you?" he asks.

"*Moi? Je suis ta mère, ta soeur, ta fille, ta femme, ta maîtresse*—Me? I am your mother, your sister, your daughter, your wife, your mistress," the jackal cackles in French.

"*Que lest votre nom?*—What is your name?" John Revell repeats, switching to French.

"*Mi nombre no es nombre. Mi nombre es tu nombre. Mi nombre es todos los nombres*—My name is no name. My name is your name. My name is all names," she declares rapidly in Spanish.

John presses harder. "*¿Cuál es tu nombre?*—What is your name?" he insists, also speaking in Spanish.

She howls. "*Yinishyé. Yinishyé*—I am called" she yells out in Navajo.

"Her name is *Azaneem*," the doctor states quietly.

"Shh. Shh. Be at peace, Jackson Fisher. She will tell us," Mathoni soothes. Dr. Fisher closes his eyes and is quiet.

"*Haash yinílyé?*—What's your name?" John asks her in the Navajo language.

"*Kahsén:na, kahsén:na, kahsén:na*—Name, name, name.*" she responds in Mohawk, "*Wá:s sera:ko tsi niká:ien íhsehre*—Go choose the one that you want."

"*Ónhka róhthare?*—Who is this speaking?" John asks, matching her language again.

"*Kahsén:na,*" she repeats.

"Tell me your name in English," John demands.

"My name is...Puddin'tame. Ask me again, I'll tell you the same," she giggles obscenely like a naughty child.

John nods at Shemnon and Jonas, who grip her more tightly around the torso, legs, and hands.

"What...is...your...name?" John demands.

"*Azaneem*. My name is *Azaneem*," she snarls.

"*Azaneem*. Whose body have you taken?" John asks.

"Some trollop. Some tramp. Some nobody. She's gone away, and you can't get her back," *Azaneem* exclaims joyfully.

"Carla. Carla Horn," Doctor whispers.

Mathoni looks up. "Her name is Carla Horn," he says.

John looks into the eyes of the woman once known as Carla. "I wish to speak with Carla Horn," he says.

"*Teietharáhkhwa teiakóhthare*—She is busy at the

175

moment," *Azaneem* mocks, again speaking in the Mohawk language. "*Iáh, ken té:iens*—No, she is not here."

"Come forth, Carla Horn. Be strong and fight her, Carla," John says.

The jackal twists and bucks, trying to escape, but the two strong men hold her firmly. At last, she seems to contract, almost as if she were a balloon leaking air. She sighs raggedly.

"Carla," John coaxes, "will you speak to me?"

The change that comes over the woman is dramatic. Her features soften, and her eyes lose the fire that is present when the evil entity is in control. Her lips quiver, and tears course down her cheeks. She looks at John helplessly.

"Carla, can you speak?" John asks.

She nods her head feebly. "Carla *ióntiats,*" she says.

He smooths her hair and cups her chin lovingly.

"*Shawátis ióntiats*—My name is John. Carla, do you wish to be released from the being that has taken possession of you?" he asks.

She nods slightly, never taking her eyes from his.

"Carla, *Enkonhshié:non*—I will help you. I am going to free you, and you will find yourself in a place of love. You will no longer feel pain. You will be at peace forever. To grant you that serenity, I must release you from your mortal bonds. Do you understand?" John says.

Carla smiles weakly and blinks her eyes.

"*Ó:nen kenh satateweienentá:'on?*—Are you ready?"

John asks, caressing her cheek tenderly.

Carla gazes gratefully at him. "*Konnorónhkhwa*," she whispers, barely audible.

"And I love you, Carla," he responds. He kisses her on the forehead and places his hands back at the sides of her face.

Mathoni touches the Trackers one by one. "Turn away, Dane. Turn away, Graham. Turn away, Lee," he directs them.

Dane obediently drops his head to his chest; Graham turns around and stares at the river; Lee closes his eyes and continues to pray.

John takes a firm hold on Carla's head. At the last moment, *Azaneem* attempts to retake possession. "*Iáh!*" She screams long and loud, but her voice is abruptly cut off as John forcefully twists Carla's head, breaking her neck.

"*Iakwáhsa'as*—We finish it. Be at peace, Carla," he says, tears streaming down his face. "Return to the Father and be at peace at last."

The once beautiful and vibrant Mohawk woman's body collapses and falls to the ground in a heap of crumbled pieces. The jackal was right: they always wear out. Shemnon and Jonas gather the remnants and take them near the river, reverently burying them in the fertile ground where once grew the lifegiving three sisters—maize, beans, and squash.

John, the Trackers, and the Nephite disciples carefully distribute Jackson Fisher's weight between themselves and slowly carry him back to the motorhome.

CHAPTER FIFTEEN
<u>THE SEEN</u>

THE WINNEBAGO MOTORHOME IS FULL, but even with its seven passengers, it is considerably more comfortable for them than John Revell's passenger van, which has been generously donated to the New York Syracuse Mission of the Church of Jesus Christ of Latter-day Saints. After John donated the van, the men, with Jackson Fisher settled into his bed in the RV, head out on the road, planning a stopover in Tennessee. This time, though, they will not avail themselves of a luxury hotel.

Shemnon, having spent more time in this vehicle and familiar with its operation, is the driver on this leg of the trip. Dane called shotgun and rides in the passenger captain's seat beside him. Graham and Jonas, the two largest men, lounge in the oversized club chairs while Lee and John sit together on the RV's couch. They have no need for stretch breaks; the deluxe motorhome is fully self-contained with toilet, shower, kitchen, and dining table, and the pantry is stocked with food.

Dr. Jackson Fisher rests peacefully on his queen-size bed in the rear of the vehicle with Mathoni sitting beside him, applying and reapplying herbal poultices to his patient's extensive wounds. The scalp laceration was not serious and is already healing, as are the 20 deep vertical tears along his torso.

His hands are the most concerning. The survey stakes were made from rough lumber, ripped into square 2x2 poles, and sharpened only enough to make them sink into the ground when hammered. Four square inches of wood were forcefully shoved through each of the doctor's palms. Bones were crushed, ligaments were shredded, and the open holes were filled with splinters. Mathoni pays the most attention to those injuries. They will mend, and it will take time; however, the doctor's recuperation will be faster because of Mathoni's supernatural healing skills. Even now the bones are knitting, and the ligaments and nerve endings are reattaching.

Mathoni wants the doctor to remain in the bed, so he shares the room with him. The jackknife couch makes into a king bed, and Lee and John will be more than comfortable sleeping there. Dane has claimed the over-the-cab bunk, and Graham will sleep in the dining area, which makes into a full bed. Shemnon and Jonas will recline the captain's seats and doze in the cab. None of them plan to leave the RV.

For the first full hour of the trip, nobody speaks. Once

the initial shock wears off, however, the Trackers are anxious to learn more about "the seen," as they call them. The Nephites, in turn, look forward to becoming more acquainted with the Trackers. Jonas cannot take his eyes from Lee, to the point where Lee begins to be uncomfortable.

"Jonas, you keep looking at me. Is there something you wish to say or to ask me?" Lee says.

"I'm sorry. I'm just fascinated about you being related to *Hiawatha*. So am I. Isn't that wild?" Jonas says. "We could trade stories."

Dane swings the passenger seat around. "No! No stories, please. If you guys want to spin yarns, go to the table and talk quietly. I'm begging you," he says.

The RV passengers are silent, and then everyone breaks into laughter. Dane takes his finger and pulls his own cheek. "Yeah, yeah, yeah. I'm a guppy. You caught me again," he says, swinging his seat back around.

Graham looks from one man to another. "I have so many questions, I don't know where to start," he says.

"Like what, Graham?" Jonas says.

"Like why and how your people came to America. What was it like back then? Did you have wives and families? That kind of thing," Graham says.

"We all had families. I am a Nephite. My father was named Nephi, my grandfather was named Nephi, and my lineage before that was Helaman, Helaman, Alma, Alma,

Nephi, and Lehi, who was descended through Abraham, Isaac, Jacob, and Joseph of Manasseh, one of the 12 tribes of Israel," Jonas says.

"Wait! Your ancestor was THE Lehi? The one who first found THE *Liahona*?" Dane asks, wide-eyed.

"That's right. Back then, I had a beautiful wife, and her name was Sarha. She was like an untamed mare, with long black hair and large dark eyes. She loved to run. She ran everywhere. I had to chase her anytime I wanted to kiss her," Jonas laughs, "and I caught her a lot. Sarha gave me ten children. The boys all looked like me—big boned, broad shouldered. But the girls. Oh, the girls. They were the image of their mother. I loved the boys, but I miss the girls the most."

"What happened to them?" Dane asks.

"Sarha eventually died, as did all my offspring, but not before they grew up and had children of their own, who had children of their own, and so forth. They were mortal, you see. All things mortal eventually perish," he says.

"Except you. You don't perish," Graham says.

"Mmmm. Well, not exactly. We will cease to exist as humans and will be instantly taken beyond the veil, but we will not know death, per se," he says.

"When Jonas, Shemnon, and Mathoni were granted their desire to remain on the earth, they were transfigured," Lee says. "They were changed from mortal beings to immortal beings. Once that occurred, they would never again suffer

181

human frailties. Am I correct in that, John?"

"Yes. That's true. Their bodies are different now. They cannot die or be injured. By the same token, they cannot father children either," John says.

"Wow. That's interesting. So, after your wife died, you never had another family," Graham says.

"That is correct. I never wanted another family. My Sarha will be waiting for me whenever I cross over," Jonas says.

Mathoni walks in from the bedroom and stands in the kitchen, joining the conversation.

"I am of Jaredite descent. My sweet wife Sakhele was Ethiopian," he says. "Her family came over on a ship like we did. They were healers and diviners. Superstitious people called them witches and devils, but they were just ordinary people who were more connected to nature. In fact, Sakhele is the one who taught me the healing arts. I fought a lot back then to protect her from simple-minded villagers. Yes, I see you looking at me like that. I may be smaller, but I'm feisty," Mathoni laughs.

"What about you, Shemnon?" Graham asks.

Shemnon glances into the rearview mirror at the men. "I am from the Lamanite tribe. My wife was a young English colonist who was captured by the Cherokee. Her name was Amelia. She had soft blond hair and light blue eyes. We lived among the Cherokee for many years during the 18th century, and then we struck out on our own and became farmers. I built

182

all the buildings myself. We had a good and simple life.

"When Amelia died, most of my children were already grown and still lived with the Cherokee. My youngest son couldn't stay on the farm by himself, so I took him back to *Qualla* to live with his brothers and other family there. His name was Shem, and I guess he was my favorite because he was the baby and had blue eyes like Amelia. After I left Shem, I continued my mission," he says.

"Wait a minute. John just said that you guys were changed before Jesus left and you wouldn't be able to have children. So how did you accomplish that almost two centuries later?" Dane says.

"I...asked for permission to be mortal for a while," Shemnon replies.

"No way," Dane says.

"As you are so fond of saying, 'yes way.' I was given the chance to be a husband and a father since I was an unmarried man when my mission began. After my wife died, God told me my time was up, and here I am...immortal again," Shemnon says.

"This is crazy," Dane says grinning. "Nobody will ever believe this."

"Nobody is ever to know, Dane...Graham...Liahona. You must not tell anyone about us. We still have work to do, and with times as they are, it would be a media feeding frenzy. You cannot even tell your wives or your children. Is that understood?" Jonas says.

The Trackers are all silent, but they each nod in agreement. They, too, know how public opinion can be warped and sensationalized.

"Kenny!" Graham blurts.

Lee sighs and purses his lips. "Chenaniah will know. Luna will tell him. He knows so much already, but if I swear him to secrecy, he will obey me," he assures them.

"You know, sometimes your abilities can be a curse as much as a blessing," John says.

"You are so right," Lee agrees.

"Well, since we're going full disclosure here, I need to ask you guys something really, really important," Dane says, swinging his seat back around.

They give Dane their full attention, waiting for his important question.

"Which one of you guys had a burger?" he asks.

Graham reaches forward and smacks Dane on the forehead. "Man, will you shut up about the burger?" he says.

Once they settle down and stop laughing, Dane gets serious. "This is for real, now. I'm not joking around. You four 'seen' guys know that we have special abilities which help us track missing persons and criminals. That's why we were chosen to come on this quest. The ancient *Liahona* gives direction, but we and our team can provide specific details that are not directional," he says, "so, here's my dilemma: I am a clairalient, also called a clairscentrist, and I pick up scents nobody else can smell. Did you know that all people carry a combination of aromas passed down from their parents?"

"I didn't know that," Graham says.

"Now you do," Dane quips.

"What are you getting at, Dane?" Lee asks.

"Let me try and explain this, Hona. Everyone has a distinctive scent profile. Part of it comes from the father, and part comes from the mother, unless there is a gifted child. That gifted child carries the exact scent combination of the gifted parent. It's like the DNA of smells. Let's use you, for example, Lee. I would say that your fragrance is like longleaf pine trees and a rich, river sediment," he says.

"That is quite complimentary," Lee says frowning.

"No, here's the point. Wren smells like..." Dane says.

"Watch it, son," Lee warns.

"Wren smells like birch bark and red clay. It's actually quite a pleasant combination. It's what I detect on you guys. But get this," he says, looking at Graham. "Gray, your wife Shine...her aroma is longleaf pine trees and red clay. She's a perfect mix of Lee and Wren, and so is her twin Cy. The other kids are different mixtures of the four elements, like twins Bill and Selah are birch bark and river sediment, twins Debby and Zorah are red clay and river sediment, Shelly is longleaf pine and birch bark. Kenny is exactly the same as Lee: longleaf pine and river sediment. Do you see what I'm saying?"

"I think I do, Dane. You can identify familial groups by their scent combinations," John says.

"Bingo! You got it, John!" Dane snaps his fingers.

"That's amazing, Dane. I get it, too, but why is this suddenly so important?" Graham says.

"Because...because," Dane says, swinging his chair to face Jonas, "you, Jonas, *also* exude the aroma of longleaf pine trees and river sediment."

"Meaning?" Jonas asks.

"Meaning, proof positive you and Lee are both gifted and share ancestors. You said it yourself when you were teasing me earlier. You're related to *Hiawatha*, so you guys are related to each other. But even more unreal is the fact that *you* had the aroma profile *before Hiawatha* was born, so *he* is *your* descendant, not the other way around. And it also means that *you*, Liahona Thistleseed, are descended from Lehi, who would have smelled like longleaf pine and river sediment!" Dane says. He swings his chair around twice, looking smug.

"Dane! That is the most incredible thing I have ever heard...other than Lee's poetic tracks and Graham's ability to echo everything he hears," John says smiling broadly. "I am quite impressed.

"You should be, John. Want to know what you smell like? Desert sand and fish. Why do you think?" Dane asks, leaning forward and cocking his head to the side quizzically.

"Because my ancestors came from the desert, and used

to be fishermen?" John says.

"Could be, John. But you know what's even wilder? Dr. Jackson Fisher smells like...desert sand and fish," Dane says.

Everyone is quiet. Lee turns his head and regards his friend. "You promised to be honest with me, John," he says.

"And I will be, Lee, now that we are all being 'seen' for who we are," John replies.

"Is Dr. Fisher your father?" Graham asks.

"The doctor and I *are* related by blood," he says, "that is one reason this quest has been so important to me. But, it's not the only reason. First of all, let me tell you that I am *not* a Nephite disciple, but I *am* a disciple of Christ."

"We know that, John. You are the Tallahassee Mission President. We are all disciples of Christ," Lee says.

"Yes, but I am one of the 12 *original* disciples of Christ. The youngest, in fact. My given name is John. In Aramaic, I was called *Yohanān Shlihā*. My father's name was Zebedee, and my mother's name was Salome.

"I had a brother named James. Jesus called us *Boanerges*—sons of thunder. My brother was the first Apostle to die as a martyr for the Savior. My family fished in the Sea of Galilee. We once caught 153 fish in one day, and we fed them to the poor.

"I, along with another disciple named Peter, was the one who made the preparation for the final Passover meal, which is known as the Last Supper. At that meal, Jesus called

187

me his beloved disciple, and I did love him well.

"I alone remained at the foot of the cross on Calvary when he was crucified. He entrusted his mother, Mary, into my care before he voluntarily gave up his life. Three days later, the Magdalene told me his burial tomb was empty, and I ran to see, but Peter entered before me and found the folded shroud.

"I was present when the Savior returned to us and showed us the marks in his hands and feet from being nailed to the cross at Golgotha and the gash in his side from the Roman soldier's sword.

"I was a teacher and a priest. Before his ascension into Heaven, I asked the Lord to allow me to stay and preach the gospel until his return to glory, and he granted my request.

"I lived for many years as an outcast on the island of Patmos, after being plunged into boiling oil in Rome. I suffered no ill effects, but every person in the Colosseum was converted to Christianity that day when they witnessed the miracle. During my time in exile on Patmos, I wrote of the revelations I was given through the Holy Ghost.

"I have been allowed to walk the earth as a ministering servant until the time of the Lord's Second Coming, just like my three Nephite brothers. Dr. Fisher is not my ancestor; he is my descendant.

"I am John the Beloved, John the Apostle, John the Revelator, and I have lived for over 2000 years," John says.

CHAPTER SIXTEEN
CHAPEL IN THE COVE

GRAHAM HEARS LEE LEAVE the RV in the wee hours of the morning while it is yet dark outside. His mentor has been tossing and turning all night, wrestling with the revelations from the previous night. Of course, Graham himself cannot sleep, as much for his conflicted feelings as for his enhanced hearing which causes every little sound to work itself into his ears. At home, he sleeps with a fan that effectively masks noises, except for the sweet murmurings his dear wife makes as she rests beside him. In an enclosed box full of men, however, there is no way to keep the noises from creeping in.

From his bed in the kitchen/dining area, he can detect the slow footfalls outside the vehicle, and soon he hears the familiar sounds of his father-in-law conversing with his God. Graham did not grow up with conventional Christianity. His religion is based on things of nature, legends, and traditions.

The RV passengers, with the exception of Dr. Fisher and himself, are men of faith in one man, this Jesus of whom they speak. Graham feels left out in a way. He remembers missionaries on the Reservation preaching about Jesus as they tried to convert the Navajo to their churches. There were many faiths, many denominations, many beliefs on what was true and what was not. Some preached forgiveness; some preached hellfire and damnation. God had many faces: He was love, he was a jealous God, he was a kind father, he was a stern taskmaster. *Which is the true face of God?* he wonders. *The answer is not in this bed*, he tells himself.

Graham quietly exits the motorhome and walks to where Lee sits on the ground. They are in North Carolina at a rest area. The weather is pleasant and somewhat warmer than upstate New York. Graham listens to the chatter of squirrels in the branches, the back-and-forth trills and whistles of the birds, the gentle breeze stirring the leaves of the trees, and he is at peace. *The face of God is here in the beauty of His world,* he decides.

"Graham, can you not sleep, son?" Lee asks.

Graham takes a seat on the soft ground beside him. "No, I'm a little too big for that bed. Thought I'd come out here and keep you company," he says.

Lee reaches over and rests his hand on Graham's thick leg. "You are a good friend, and I am so blessed to have you as my son-in-law. Thank you," he says.

Graham places his large paw over his friend's hand. "And I will never stop being grateful that you are both my friend and my sweet wife's father," he says.

"It has been quite a journey, has it not? What are your impressions now that we have experienced all these new phenomena?" Lee asks.

Graham exhales heavily. "I don't know if I will ever be surprised again. Who could've expected this turn of events? I thought that monsters of sand were the pinnacle of my life experiences. I was wrong. I hope nothing surpasses this quest. I don't think I could survive it," he says.

Lee chuckles. "Yes, you can. You are the strongest man I have ever met, not just physically, but within your heart. I can hardly wait for February," he says.

"Ah, yes. Natalie's anticipated arrival. You will be a grandfather, and I will be a daddy. I can hardly believe it will be here so soon. Lee, I give you my word right here and now that I will love and protect and provide for your daughter and our children with all that I have within me for the rest of my natural life," Grahams vows.

Lee pats his leg. "I know you will, son. I know. And that eases my mind more than you will ever know. Well, look. The sun is coming up. I do not know about you, but I am quite hungry. Shall we try to rustle up some breakfast before the others wake?" he says.

"I think as soon as we try, they will all wake up, and the first one will be our resident bloodhound, Inspector Lightfoot," Graham laughs.

And they are absolutely correct. No sooner do they ignite the propane eye on the stovetop than they hear Dane's head hit the ceiling of the cab as he sits up in his bunk.

"Ow. Scrambled for me, please," Dane calls.

"Haven't even had the chance to crack an egg," Graham whispers.

"Hey. Don't have to have psychic hearing to know what you said, dude," Dane says. "I'll have three on toast."

Lee and Graham find themselves the breakfast chefs. The patriarch of a huge family, Lee is used to cooking in bulk and often helps Wren out in the kitchen. In no time, the three Trackers and the four disciples devour two dozen scrambled eggs, toast, jelly, and orange juice. Thankfully, the only cleanup involves washing the pan because the doctor keeps a supply of paper and plastics which fill the garbage bag.

Nobody speaks of the prior evening's bombshells, and the conversation is centered on where they plan to go today.

"Aren't we heading home?" Dane asks.

"Sorry, Dane, but this quest is not over. Now that we've eaten, we need to consult the compass," John says.

"*Our* Liahona or the *other Liahona*?" Dane asks.

"Your Compass needs to consult the other compass," Jonas replies.

Lee removes the *Liahona* from the velveteen bag and holds it in his cupped hands. The spindles begin revolving. When they stop, the writing appears inside the ball. John reads the words. "Cades Cove Loop," he says, "Not surprised. I'd already thought we might go back to Tennessee."

"Y'all really like Tennessee, don't you?" Graham says.

"We do," John laughs. "There's something wholesome and fresh and clean about that area. Well, let's get going."

Lee is surprised to find that they are only 45 minutes from their destination. Turning onto Little River Road, they drive for about 25 miles before coming to the entrance of Cades Cove Loop Road, a one-way paved road that circles the Cove.

"Where do we go?" Graham asks.

"It didn't say," John responds. "I think we cruise until we receive a sign to stop. It's a beautiful driving tour, so pull up the blinds and keep your eyes open for deer and bears."

"Oh, more bears!" Dane exclaims, pressing his face against the large picture window. Graham and Lee join him, and soon the three of them are rubbernecking, hoping to spot bears and other wildlife. Shemnon drives slowly along the Loop Road, affording his passengers every opportunity to view the historic cabins and outbuildings in their natural settings.

The bedroom door opens, and Mathoni enters the room carrying two empty paper plates. "He's eating quite well, and I believe he might like to get out and stretch his legs soon," he says.

Inside the bedroom, Dr. Fisher hears him. "I'd like to get out and stretch my legs soon," he calls. The others laugh, relieved that he is healing so quickly.

"Mathoni, you are incredible. Thank you," John says.

"It is not my skill that is healing him, John. It's out of my hands," Mathoni says.

"And it's this place," Shemnon says. "It's special to him. Many memories. The longer we stay, the better he will become. That's why I am driving so slowly. I see in the mirror that he has opened not just the shades, but the window opposite his bed. The very air renews him. The *Liahona* was right to direct us here. God knows what Dr. Fisher needs."

John, Mathoni, and Jonas turn and look back into the motorhome. The Trackers are glued to the picture window, and the doctor has scooted to the end of his bed and sits with his elbows on the shelf in front of his window. It is indeed a place of renewal for all of them.

"Look, look," Dr. Fisher shouts. "It's the walkway to the old Methodist Church. Pull over, please. I'd really like to go inside. It was one of my family's favorite stops."

John and the Nephites smile at one another. It is the sign for which they are waiting. Shemnon pulls the RV to the far-left side of the road and parks.

"We're getting out?" Dane asks excitedly.

"We're getting out, but don't wander away. Please stay together children," John says.

Instead of being offended, the Trackers simply grin as they tumble outside into the cool, crisp air. Mathoni walks Dr. Fisher to the door, and Jonas lifts him down.

"I can walk. What's your name again?" he says.

"My name's Joe, and these are my friends Matt and Jim," Jonas says.

"And I'm John. We've been taking care of you since yesterday when we found you at the Mohawk reservation," John says. "Do you remember?"

"Tell you the truth, I don't. I think I fell down or was mugged or something. I've got some serious cuts and abrasions to my hands and torso, but they seem to be healing satisfactorily. This one—Matt—has done an excellent job of cleaning and bandaging the wounds," he says.

"Yes, Matt has some medical training. EMT, I believe. He's quite good," Jonas says.

"I've got to thank you, Matt. You've done wonders with my injuries," Dr. Fisher says.

"It has been my privilege, Dr. Fisher," Matt responds.

"Oh! Iris nevi," the doctor says as he looks into Matt's eyes. "You have iris nevi. Eye freckles. Usually they present as dark spots, but yours are different. I've never seen these silver striations before. Quite striking. Runs in families, you know."

"Is that a fact? I never gave it much thought," Matt says, "but you're right. All my children have them."

"Learn something new and interesting every day, huh.

It's a really good thing you found me when you did. Otherwise, my cuts might have gotten infected. Oh, hey, there's the three other guys. Tell me again why you seven men are together and why you're traveling in my motorhome," he says as they begin making their way slowly up the church walk.

"We are a Bible study group on a men's retreat. Our church van broke down at the reservation, and we were taking a walk around when we found you lying unconscious at that construction site. Matt doctored you up, and you asked us to ride back to Florida with you," John says.

"Did I? I suppose I must have. Well, like I said, I'm glad you found me. I've been a little lost lately, but I've got to get back to my practice," Fisher says.

"What kind of practice?" Shemnon asks.

"Didn't I tell you? I'm a plastic surgeon. I sure hope my hands heal up. They're my livelihood, you know. By the way, where's your church van?" he says.

"Totally conked out. Engine blew. We can't afford to buy another one yet. That's why we're so glad you were kind enough to offer us a ride home," Jonas says.

"Sure thing. Here we are. The Methodist Church. Built in 1820. Can you even conceive of what it must have been like back then?" Fisher asks.

"I can only imagine," John smiles.

The eight men enter the whitewashed wooden church building through one of the two side-by-side front doors, which were meant to separate the men from the women in the congregation. The doors open into two aisles which flank a center section of pews and two outer sections. At the back wall is a raised pulpit area on which sits a small carved wooden podium, bordered on either side by two matching carved pedestals. A single pew rests along the wall behind the podium, and an old upright piano stands perpendicular to it on the left.

A simple, unadorned wooden cross hangs on the wall above the pew. To the left, behind and parallel to the piano, are three rows of long wooden pews which extend to the wall. An identical configuration is opposite, behind and to the right of the raised area. The arrangement of pews forms a U-shape around an open expanse of the floor in front of the podium. John walks unassisted to the front and stands in the open area.

"Did you know I was married in this church?" he asks.

"No, you did not tell us that," Lee says.

"I was. My fiancé Cheryl and I came up here to get married. We were just going to do the Justice of the Peace thing, but we visited here and fell in love with this church. We already had our license, so we stopped at the Ranger Station on the way out and found somebody who was a Notary Public. He came back with us and performed the service on the spot. One of the happiest days of my life," Fisher says tearfully, sitting down on the platform.

Mathoni approaches the doctor and touches his shoulder. "Be at peace, Jackson Fisher," he says.

The doctor stops crying and drops his chin, resting it on his chest. Mathoni places his hands gently on the man's head. Shemnon and Jonas also step up and place their hands on his head. John ascends the platform and seats himself at the old piano. He begins to play a song. The tune is driving and masculine, with ornamentation reminiscent of Israeli folk songs. And then, the three Nephite disciples begin to sing.

We have walked the earth for generations without end.
We may be a stranger; we may even be a friend.
We are like the angels as we minister to all
as the Lord intends.
Great and marvelous the message that we tell.
Everlasting life for all families, as well,
in the Father's Kingdom with Jesus they'll dwell.
All shall blessed be.
No more shall they taste of death or pain.
Glory in His Kingdom evermore remain.
Go and preach the gospel,
turn the souls of men back to God again.
I would tarry 'til You come to earth, O Lord.
I would tarry 'til You come again.
I would travel o'er the land to preach Your word
of salvation for all men.

"Lee," Graham whispers.

"Shhh. Yes. I know. Chenaniah told me of Maria's dream. These are the three singers she heard," Lee says.

The Nephite disciples continue standing around Jackson Fisher. John descends the platform and rests his hands atop theirs.

"Jackson Fisher. From this day forward, you will be at peace with your profession and with your life. You will no longer take pleasure in gambling for money or placing bets and wagers. You will live according to your divine purpose, which is to provide help and healing to those who need your special gifts. You will love yourself and your family, and you will forget the evils which have befallen you. We give you this blessing in the most Holy name of Jesus Christ. Amen," John says.

Throughout the prayer, the Trackers bow their heads and close their eyes, including Graham. As soon as John stops speaking, a commotion at the front doors draws their attention.

An exuberant three-year-old boy runs into the church. He stops, confused for a moment, and then he darts past the Trackers and throws himself into Jackson Fisher's lap.

"Jackie! Jackie! Come back here. Don't you run away from me," a young woman calls. She enters the church and stops dead in her tracks. "Mom! Mom! Come quick!"

A salt-and-pepper-haired woman of 58 rushes into the room. She, too, stops short seeing the child in the doctor's lap.

"Jack? What...what are...what are you doing here?" she stammers.

The doctor stares open mouthed at her and the young woman. "Cheryl? Katelyn?" he says.

199

"Dad? I don't understand," Katelyn says.

"Peepaw," the little boy shouts, throwing his arms around Fisher's neck, "I you Jackie, Peepaw."

A young man in his early 20s enters, "What's the problem, Katelyn? Whoa. Dad is that you?" he says.

"Frankie?" the doctor whispers.

"Peepaw," Jackie says, squeezing his little arms around Fisher's neck tightly.

"We were vacationing, and the kids wanted to come back here. It was our place, you know," Cheryl says, her voice shaking. "Why are you here?"

"I…was…hmm. Not sure. I think I was vacationing as well, but I had some sort of mishap. Cut my hands." He holds up his bandaged hands. "These four guys found me, and…um…they're catching a ride back to Tallahassee in my RV. Is that right, guys?" he asks, looking around at John and the Trackers.

It is not until that moment that the Trackers realize there are only four of them in the room. The three Nephite disciples are again unseen. Lee catches John's eye.

"That's correct, Dr. Fisher. We are so grateful for your generosity, and as soon as we get back, we'll be able to reimburse you for your troubles," John says.

"Nonsense. You helped me; I help you. These are my family. Cheryl and my kids, Katelyn and Frankie, and I guess this is my grandson. Jackie?" he says.

Katelyn's chin trembles. "I named him after you, Dad. Jackson Fisher Keyman. My name's Keyman now," she says.

Tears spill down the doctor's face. "He's perfect, honey. He's perfect in every way," he says, drawing the child closer in a warm embrace.

Cheryl edges closer. "Jackie, honey," she says, "how did you know this was your Peepaw?"

"The man told me," he says.

"One of these men told you?" she questions.

"No, Meemaw. The man what gots sparkly eyes," Jackie says, laying his head against Jackson's neck, "Jackie love you, Peepaw."

Katelyn runs forward and throws her arms around the two of them, and Frankie follows suit. "We miss you, Dad. Every day, we miss you," the young man says.

Cheryl tentatively approaches them. Jackson Fisher extends his hand to Cheryl, who gingerly takes it. He stands up, still cradling little Jackie, and folds her into the group hug.

"We all miss you, Jack," she sobs.

John and the Trackers withdraw out the door and stand on the stoop. They are all crying and not caring who notices.

John puts his arm around Lee's shoulders. "They're gone, you know, and they've taken the *Liahona* with them. There are other missions for them to see to. This one has almost reached its happy conclusion," he says.

"Will the doctor be healed? Can he perform surgery?"

Lee asks with concern.

"You need no longer worry, Lee. Sali Mata will be made whole. I promise you," John says, "and I stand by my word. Come, let's wait for the Fishers at the RV. They have much catching up to do to mend their family unit. And besides, Graham and Dane look like they're starving."

* * *

At their Tallahassee home, Chenaniah Thistleseed and Arfang sat lazily in the glider in the shade of the morning glory covered pergola over the back patio. Both boys had purple mouths from the grape popsicles they had just consumed. Arfang opened his mouth wide and Kenny erupted into laughter at the sight of his purple tongue sticking out. The two were no longer strangers.

We are not so different, Kenny thought to his friend Luna, *and I admire him.*

You are right, Chenaniah. You two are much the same, Luna thought back to him.

Kenny grinned and regarded his new little brother. He really did admire him. He admired Arfang's unbridled sense of humor, and he admired Arfang's courage after the villagers massacred his family. But more than anything, he admired Arfang's amazing eyes with their silver streaks…just like his sister Sali Mata's.

* * *

In a small room in the Tallahassee Long-Term Care

Facility, a man lay in his bed. He had been there for several years. His chest, arms, and one leg were badly scarred. His face and head on one side were red and shiny where the skin and hair had been burned off. Though he was often in a minimally conscious or semiconscious state, his eyelids fluttered open from time to time, and his pale blue eyes flitted around the room as if searching for someone or something. He began taking erratic breaths, lost in a waking nightmare.

A dark-haired male nurse in maroon scrubs stood beside the bed, listening to the sounds of his patient's 3breathing. He reached down and gently passed his hand over the man's eyes. "Be at peace," he said quietly. The man's eyes closed, and his breathing became regular again. The nurse nodded to the patient's visitor.

The visitor opened the drawer of the small night table beside the bed and checked to make sure the contents were still there. Inside were the only possessions the patient had with him when he was brought to this facility: a large Bowie knife, a charred yellow hair ribbon, and a gar fish jaw on a necklace of braided sinew. He closed the drawer and sat quietly in a nearby chair.

"You will be made whole soon, blood of my blood. Until then, I would tarry with you," Shemnon said.

EPILOGUE

<u>THE KEEPER</u>

I FINISH collecting the story of Liahona—the Compass. I am very tired, but my fears are gone. The sun is high overhead. My body is covered with sweat from the journey, but Mother has shaded my face with her body. I open my eyes and hear her sigh of relief.

Luna," Mother says. "My daughter. *Que Pasa?* How are you? *Enkv?* OK?"

I am used to the odd mix of Spanish, English, and Muskogee in her conversation.

"*Si, Mama.* All is well with my friend's father and the rest of his family," I say.

"What do you keep?" Mother asks.

"My friend's new sister will be made whole, and soon there will be more nieces and nephews," I say with a smile.

She nods her head at me. "You were very fearful this time, weren't you?" she asks.

"Yes, I was. I was afraid for my friend's father because I could not know the hearts of these other men, but his own power and heart were great, and he now knows what is beyond the veil of death," I say.

"*Mvdo*. It is good. *Andale*. Let's go" she says. Mother takes my hand and walks me toward our village. I am grateful for her strong, but tender touch.

"How long, Mother?" I ask.

"Only one day this time, daughter," Mother says, "It is as before. You are gone one day for each week. When it happens, I have much fear for you, Luna." She pulls me close and kisses my cheek.

We walk silently for a while. "Mother, I am sometimes afraid, too," I admit.

"Have you seen something troubling?" she asks.

I don't answer right away. I am troubled, for I know there will be a journey in the future that will not end so well. "Yes. As always, danger surrounds these people. I am never sure what will happen," I say.

Mother pulls me close and pats my hand as we continue walking. "Do not worry, Luna," she says. "I know that you are a *hecetv*—a seer. You will see whatever will be. And you will give your friend the guidance he needs to help his people be victorious in all their challenges."

"There will be a dangerous time for my brother and the woman he loves," I say.

"Which of your brothers?" Mother asks.

"My brother Noah," I say.

"Ah, Noah," Mother says.

"His chosen mate will be sorely tested," I say, "and he will be tested with her."

"Yes, but as you always say, 'they are strong together.' Is that not right?" Mother says.

"It is. But will their strength be enough to overcome the peril they must face? That is my great fear," I say.

APPENDIX

LANGUAGE TRANSLATIONS

Mohawk Language

Kanien'kéha is a language of the Iroquoian family which is spoken in Canada and New York State. It has relatively few letters in its alphabet, but they are combined to make extremely long words. As a tonal language, the upward and downward vocal inflections are crucial to the meaning of the words. Slight differences in pronunciation exists between the Canadian and United States dialects. A basic outline follows.

Vowels are pronounced as follows:

ORAL vowels are openly voiced. Like vowels are pronounced the same, but their TONES can be rising or falling. A RISING tone is voiced with a rising pitch and is indicated by an upward diacritical mark. A FALLING tone is voiced with a falling pitch and is indicated by a downward diacritical mark.		
A=w*A*tch	À=falling tone	Á=rising tone
E=b*E*d or bUd *(guttural inflection)*	È=falling tone	É=rising tone
I =b*EE*t or b*A*d *(nasalized)*	Ì=falling tone	Í=rising tone
O=g*O* or g*OO*d *(nasalized)*	Ò=falling tone	Ó=rising tone
NASALIZED vowels let air pass through the nose.		
DIPTHONGS (two vowels voiced together) follow the general rules of individual vowel voicing.		

Consonants are sounded as follows:

H=_Hair_	K=_Kick_	N=_Now_
R=_huRRah_	S=_See_	T or D=_Den_
W or U=_Wet_	TS=_haTS_	Th=_Den_
Wh=_Fat_	SH=_See_ + _He_ (voiced separately, not blended)	TSH= _haTS_ + _He_ (voiced separately, not blended)
'=glottal stop	:=slight break between words (visually separates nouns, objects, and pronouns)	

Kanien'kéha (Mohawk) Words, Phrases, and their Meanings

(in order of appearance)

Hiawatha - a great Mohawk leader and long-pine chieftain

Skennenrahawi – the Great Peacemaker

Haudenosaunee – Iroquois Confederacy

Tasatáweiat - come in

Kwe - hi

Shé:kon - hello

Skennenkó:wa ken? - How are you?

Iakentiohkowá:nen nón:wa ken' í:iens - There are a lot of people here today

Ióntiats - my name is

Wa'thiátera'ne - where those two met each other

Kanien'kehá:ka - people of the flint

Akwesasne - land where the partridge drums

O'nenste - maize

Kvja'ko'wa - big fish

Kanónhsa - house

Kanhoha - glass door

Ahtahkwa'ón:we - moccasins

Asenatara'—You should make a visit.

Ó:nen. - goodbye

Kanien'kéha – Mohawk language

Deganawida – another name for the Great Peacemaker

Tsikonsaseh - an elder known for her wise counsel

Atotarhoh - an Onondaga leader of great savagery.

Iák kenh tesahterón:ni? - Aren't you afraid?

Kahsén:na - name

Wá:s sera:ko tsi niká:ien íhsehre - Go choose the one that you want

Ónhka róhthare? - Who is this speaking?

Teietharáhkhwa teiakóhthare - She is busy at the moment

Iáh - no

Ken té:iens - she is not here

Shawátis ióntiats - My name is John

Enkonhshié:non - I will help you

Ó:nen kenh satateweienentá:'on? - Are you ready?

Konnorónhkhwa - I love you

Iakwáhsa'as - We finish it

Navajo Language

The Navajo language is spoken extensively on the Navajo Reservations. It was used by the Navajo Code Talkers in the war to send specially-coded messages to the Allied troops and was never decoded by the enemy. It is a tonal language, with unusual spellings and numerous diacritical marks that change the meanings of the words. A basic outline follows.

Vowels are pronounced as follows:

ORAL vowels are openly voiced		A=w_Atch_
E= b_Ed_	I =b_It_	O=g_O_
AA=j_AW_	EE=th_EY_	II=s_EE_
OO=g_O_ (but held longer)		AI=H_awAIi_
AO=m_AYO_	EI=_EI_ght	OI=ch_EWY_
NASALIZED vowels are made by letting air pass through the nose and are indicated by a nasal mark beneath the vowel: ą ę į ǫ		
TONES can be high or low. A HIGH tone is voiced with a raised pitch and is indicated by a diacritical mark above it: á, é, í, ó, ń, áá, éé, íí, óó Note: n is sometimes voiced as a vowel		
Two vowels of differing TONES glide together as rising or falling tones (as in Oh_IO_ – a rising/falling tone)		
Note: Nasalized vowels can also be doubled and high tones		

Consonants are sounded as follows:

B=_Boy_	D=_Door_	DL=a_D Lib_
DZ=ai_DS_	_G_=_Gun_	G=_CH_ew
H=_Hair_	J=_Joy_	K=_Ki_ck
KW=_QUi_ck	L=_Like_	M=_Man_

211

N=_N_ow	S=_S_ee	SH=_SH_e
T=_T_ime	TS=ha_TS_	W=_W_et
Y=_Y_es	Z=_Z_oo	ZH=a_Z_ure
Some consonants have no English equivalent. They are as follows:		Ł=*voiced as though saying HL together*
TŁ=_Te_L_epathy_ (*T and L voiced as one sound*)	T'=glottalized(*as in hu', two, three, four*)	TS'=glottalized (*as in wha_TS_ up*)
K'=glottalized (*as in hi_CC_up*)	CH'=glottalized (*as in what _CH_a doing*)	TŁ'=glottalized (*as in _Te_L_epa_thy*)
Notes regarding H: An *H* sound that follows *S* is written as *X* to avoid confusion with the symbol *SH* and the *H* is voiced with breath. An *H* at the end of a syllable or word is voiced with breath.		

Navajo Words, Phrases, and their Meanings

(in order of appearance)

Asdz Nádleehé – Changing Woman

Ahił danihidzul – We are strong together

Yé'iitsoh – Big Giant Monster

Yinishyé - I am called

Haash yinílyé? – What's your name?

Spanish Language

Conversational Spanish, in its many forms and dialects, is one of the most widely spoken languages in the world and is prevalent throughout Mexico, Central America, and the United States. Though it varies slightly by regions, it is generally consistent in its pronunciation.

The vowels are pronounced as follows:

A=w_A_tch	E= b_E_d	I =s_EE_
O=m_OA_n	U=b_OO_k	Y =s_EE_
Note: vowels are voiced with open, relaxed mouth.		

Consonants are sounded as follows:

B =_B_ed	C=_C_ow	C=_S_ow
D=_Th_ink	F=_F_un	G=_G_un
H=silent	J=_Ch_ew	K=_K_ick
L=_L_ick	LL=_Y_ard	M=_M_an
N=_N_ow	Ñ=can_Y_on	P=_P_ark
Q/QU=_K_ick	R=ca_RR_y	RR=as _R_, but trilled
T=_T_ake	V=_B_ed	W=_W_ater
X=e_X_cuse	Y=_Y_es	Z=pin_TS_
Note: consonants are voiced with open, relaxed mouth. Hard consonants are explosively voiced.		

Spanish Words, Phrases, and their Meanings

(in order of appearance)

Ojos del Luna - Eyes of the Moon (proper name)

Mi nombre no es nombre - My name is no name

Mi nombre es tu nombre - My name is your name

Mi nombre es todos los nombres - My name is all names

¿Cuál es tu nombre? - What is your name?

Que Pasa - what is happening?

Si, Mama - Yes, mother

Andale - let us go

Muskogee Creek Language

The Muskogee Creek language is spoken extensively on the reservations in Oklahoma; however, in the Southeast, there are relatively few native speakers. In the tri-state region of Florida, Georgia, and Alabama, language classes are held in an effort to keep the language from becoming extinct.

The vowels are pronounced as follows:

A=w_A_tch	E=_I_tch	E=s_EE_
I=s_AY_	O=m_OA_n	U=b_OO_k
V=_U_nder	EU=_U_se	UE=b_OY_
VO=n_OW_	Note: vowels are voiced with partially closed, tight mouth.	

Consonants are sounded as follows:

C=ri_CH_	C= ca_TS_	C=_J_am
F=_F_air	H=_H_air	K=bi_K_e
K=_G_o	L=_L_ike	M=_M_an
N=ma_N_	P=_P_ie	P=_B_uy
R=_TLH_ or _HL_ (There is no English equivalent. The sound is much like an attempt to bring forth phlegm)		
S=_S_ee	S= _Z_oo	SK=wi_SH_
SS=wi_SH_	T=_T_ea	T=_D_ie
W=_W_et	Y=_Y_et	
Note: Consonants are voiced with tight mouths, far back in the throat. The sounds are almost "swallowed."		

Muskogee Words, Phrases, and their Meanings

(in order of appearance)

Tvfolv – town (small town with one mound)

Enkv – O.K., all right

Mvdo – It is well; it is good; good; thank you; you're welcome

Hecetv – you see

Other Words, Phrases, and their Meanings

Ugunyi - *(Cherokee)* the terrible

Qualla Boundary - *(Cherokee)* official name of Indian Reservation in Cherokee, NC

Adanelá tsunilawisdi - *(Cherokee)* meeting longhouse

Asi - *(Cherokee)* house

Ishtaboli - *(Choctaw)* stick ball game

Kachina - *(Hopi)* carved wooden deity figurine

Isa Naja - *(Mandinkan)* Jesus, come down

Isa be kanuring - *(Mandinkan)* Jesus loves you

Isa ben kanuring - *(Mandinkan)* Jesus loves me

Bonjour - *(French)* Hello

Fleur de lis - *(French)* a white-petaled flower design

Moi - *(French)* me

Je suis ta mère - *(French)* I am your mother

ta soeur - *(French)* your sister

ta fille - *(French)* your daughter

ta femme - *(French)* your wife

ta maîtresse - *(French)* your mistress

Que lest votre nom? - *(French)* What is your name?"

Yohanān Shlihā - *(Hebrew/Aramaic)* disciple John's name

Boanerges - *(Hebrew/Aramaic)* sons of thunder

PREVIEW the NEXT BOOK in

Mickey MorningGlory's sequence of

paranormal suspense adventures!

ANDALUSITE

The Catcher's Story

Book 6 of

The TRACKERS SERIES

* * *

PROLOGUE

TALLAHASSEE, FL~JULY~1993

THE TINY BRASS BELL over the Tallahassee shopkeeper's door tinkles gently. The jewelry artisan gets to her feet and moves toward the sound. But, before she even reaches the door, she is struck hard on the back of the skull with a ballpeen hammer.

The assailant steps over the woman's body and casually approaches her worktable. It is strewn with lengths of gold and silver wire, claw fasteners, clasps, delicate jewelry crafting tools, and semi-precious stones of all colors, sizes, and shapes in miniature plastic bags and metal containers. The thief rifles through the packets and tins, searching for specific gemstones. Not finding them, he begins pulling out the small individual drawers in the wooden chest beside the table.

Opening a side door in the cabinet, he finds additional drawers. These contain the more expensive jewels: diamond baguettes, emerald chips, faceted round rubies, pale blue aquamarines, black seed pearls, white cultured pearls, and other treasures. In the bottom drawer he discovers the prize: rough and polished Andalusites. He lifts one stone up to the light and marvels at the myriad colors it produces: yellow, orange, green, brown, gold, red—a crystal filled with autumn.

He opens a battered leather valise and empties the contents of all the drawers into it...except for the Andalusites. He puts those carefully in their own separate velveteen bag.

Moving behind the display counter, he leans down and gathers all the jewels in the case. He opens the cash register, lifts out the tray, and collects the written special orders, leaving the cash and checks behind. Then, he turns to leave.

As he approaches the woman, she moans. He stands over her for a few seconds, turning his head from side to side as a curious pup does when it listens. He bends down and slams the hammer into her forehead before exiting the shop.

There are more of the misplaced stones he must find,

and Tallahassee has a lot of jewelry stores. What's more, some of the customers on these and other special work orders have had custom pieces created with his missing Andalusite gems.

* * *

At the home of Liahona and Wren Thistleseed, the family and friends gather in the breakfast room.

"...dear, Kenny. Happy birthday to you," they sing.

When the singing is over, Chenaniah Thistleseed, the family's youngest son, steps to the table and regards the burning candles on the cake—a full sheet pan two-layer chocolate chip confection with homemade dark chocolate ganache icing. He counts the candles, just to make sure they are right. Thirteen in all. He is finally a teenager. He takes a deep breath and blows, easily extinguishing all of them.

"Yay, Kenny," his little sister Shelly exclaims, "now you get your wish. What was your wish?"

"I wished..." Kenny says.

The answers ricochet like bullets around the room from his brothers and sisters. This is a Thistleseed family tradition for their birthdays.

"...to grow into those feet," his sister Shinehah says.

"...for that thing on your lip to become a mustache," her twin Cyrus says.

"...to skip acne and the other ails of becoming a teen," Jubal says.

"...to have a girlfriend before you're 50 years old,"

Bill's twin Selah says.

"...for enough money to even date a girl, provided you find one," Deborah says.

"...to learn every language in the world," her twin Zipporah says.

There is a pause, and everyone looks at Shelly for her prediction. She bites her lip and stares at the floor, and then she lifts her head and opens her eyes wide.

"...to finally be a real Tracker," she says with a grin.

"Shelly wins. That was my wish. You get the first piece of cake, Shel," Kenny says, cutting a generous square from the corner with the most icing.

After Shelly is served, Wren steps in and divides up the rest of the cake for the family and guests, and there are many. All the Trackers and their families are present: Dane and Raven Lightfoot, their twin babies Perry and Buck, and mother-in-law Robin Looking Bird; Shine's husband Graham Skysong; Jubal's wife Sali Mata and her little brother Arfang Jacomba; Noah Lightfoot and his girlfriend Maria Ramirez.

"Attention, please," Lee Thistleseed says. "As you know, today is Chenaniah's thirteenth birthday. And now, I am proud to announce that today, my son has officially become a Tracker. Congratulations, Chenaniah!"

Kenny bows magnanimously amid the thunderous applause, hoots, and hollers. Lee holds up his hands for quiet.

"What you do not know is this: today, Maria Ramirez

has officially become a Beacon for the Trackers Team! Congratulations, Maria!" Lee announces.

More applause ensues. Maria breaks into a radiant smile and lifts her arms in a victory pose.

"Hold it! Wait just a minute! No way!" shouts Selah.

The room is silent, and everyone looks back and forth at the two young women. Maria pins her arms at her side, embarrassed.

"What is wrong, dear?" Wren asks in alarm.

Selah punches Noah in the arm. "Oh, shut UP! You sneaky snake, you!" she gushes.

"What is going on, Noah?" Lee asks the young man.

Noah steps up and puts his arm around Maria. "Well, um, we weren't going to say anything yet—at least until after cake—but, um, well I, um. Oh, well, here," he hems and haws. Then, he lifts Maria's left hand in the air and shows off her custom made antique gold ring. It is set with a beautiful polished Andalusite gemstone and matches her Andalusite rosary bracelet.

"They're engaged!" scream the girls Debby, Zorah, and Selah in unison.

*　*　*

Hundreds of miles away, my eyes fly open, and I stare at nothing. I know the girl who wears the engagement ring. She is the betrothed of my brother, Noah.

I am Luna—short for *Ojos del Luna* (as my village

family calls me); *Hvresse Torwv* (as my Creek Indian mother calls me). Both names mean the same—Moon Eyes. My eyes are so blue they are almost white, and Mother tells me that is why I am blind. But when I play my flute in my dream travels, I can see over great distances. My dream world is vivid and colorful, with keen sensory perceptions of sound and smell.

I am a "Story Keeper." I remember in great detail what I see on my journeys. The stories I tell are not mine, but I keep them in my memory always, as do I keep all the other stories related to this group of people whose lives intersect mine in a strange and unexplainable way.

This one is hers—the Catcher's story. It begins the day my brother pledges himself to her with a ring and bracelet crafted from stolen and smuggled gemstones.

Continue the saga with

ANDALUSITE

The Catcher's Story

Book 6 of The TRACKERS SERIES

Patent Print Books

www.patentprintbooks.com

www.amazon.com

ABOUT THE AUTHOR

MICKEY MORNINGGLORY is a former schoolteacher, storyteller, and performer. Her diverse background includes the *American Federation of Television and Radio Artists (AFTRA)*, *Apalachicola Band of Eastern Creek Indians,* theater, civic light opera, and ethnomusicology. She is a member of *Sisters in Crime (SinC), Society of Children's Book Writers and Illustrators (SCBWI), American Copy Editors Society (ACES),* and *National Association of Independent Writers and Editors (NAIWE).*

Ms. MorningGlory's association with indigenous Native tribes has made her *"a friend of many fires."* She crafts <u>The Trackers Series</u> multicultural paranormal mystery books from her writing studio in Northwest Florida. Readers can visit her website at mickeymorningglory-us.com.

www.ingramcontent.com/pod-product-compliance
Lightning Source LLC
Chambersburg PA
CBHW020728210626
46807CB00016B/505